RAVELLED

and other stories

Sue Hampton

TSL Publications

ublished in Great Britain in 2016
L Publications, Rickmansworth

ISBN / 978-1-911070-30-6

Front cover:
detail from a portrait of the author by Sheelagh Frew Crane
Design: Mark Crane

Back cover:
portrait of Sue Hampton by Sheelagh Frew Crane
Design: Mark Crane

DEDICATION

to Mary, née Sheppard,
my longest-serving, multi-talented and generous friend,
who knows the true story behind *Ravelled*.

CONTENTS

Introduction 7

The Boarder – Reviews 9

The Boarder 11

Away for Christmas – Reviews 23

Away for Christmas 24

If – Reviews 51

If 52

Ravelled – Reviews 56

Ravelled 58

The Goddess – Reviews 74

The Goddess 75

Sid's New Start – Reviews 87

Sid's New Start 88

Sky Lady – Reviews 102

Sky Lady 103

Included – Reviews 119

Included 120

The Brute and the Beast – Reviews 129

The Brute and the Beast 130

Acknowledgements & About the Author 148

About the Authors who have reviewed stories
    in this collection 151

Introduction

I've read plenty of fine short stories in my life, including Chekhov's, and remember being impressed by Kate Atkinson's *Not the End of the World*, but although I have more than twenty novels in print, I might never have written a collection of my own without the intervention of Dr. Who!

While never a huge fan, I do remember from my childhood the black-and-white episodes with Brigadier Lethbridge-Stewart as back-up. When Candy Jar, publishers of my YA novel *Thinner than Water*, asked me to write a short story for a collection about the Brig, I was eventually won round by the premise of a first love story. Called *In His Kiss*, it took me into territory that was disconcertingly new, but proved enormous fun. This set me off exploring the short story: what it can and can't do, whether there are rules and how different it is from the novel form. My research included Margaret Atwood and Alice Munro, along with the Magic Oxygen Literary Prize Anthology (from my Green publishers for *Flashback and Purple* and *The Dreamer*) which was released with helpful timing. After a blog post to clarify my thinking, I began writing, hoping I'd learned something from the greats.

Of course I wanted to attempt various kinds of story with a range of moods. There's no sci-fi here and no crime either, but there are several styles as well as genres. You'll find a kind of fable, originally a postscript to my YA alopecia novel *Crazy Daise*, and a fairy-tale variation on *Beauty and the Beast* with a nod to *Jane Eyre*, but the rest are very much real-world stories about relationships and feelings because for me there's nothing more fascinating. I hope you'll laugh, but also cry.

I'm grateful to everyone, not just the authors but those avid readers from all over the world, who chose a story and offered a review (too many in the end to include them all). One of those readers wrote this, which seems a good way to end my introduction:

> *I always think of a book of short stories as a delicious indul-*
> *gence, something you can dip in and out of, something that*

gives you a real flavour of an author and is a great way of trying someone new before committing yourself to a novel! What a fantastic idea if it was mandatory for all published authors to include an anthology of short stories amongst their catalogue. As for **The Boarder**, *I wouldn't want to rush too quickly onto the next Sue Hampton story. My mind is still full of the last one.*

Havoc Files 2, including my story *In His Kiss*, will be published by Candy Jar around the same time as this collection.

Sue Hampton http://www.suehamptonauthor.co.uk/

You can find out more about the authors* who have read and reviewed a story in this collection at the end of the book.

The Boarder *is such a thought-provoking tale; few of us know everything there is to know about our parents, but it is always after they have left us that we start to wonder about the missing years, what were they really like as a child, were they happy, were there secrets? And all of us, when we lose somebody, still see them around us wherever we look, whether in a white feather on the ground, their human 'double' or 'the butterfly thing' which the author so beautifully describes. This is a lovely short story, sensitively and intelligently written.*

Jackie Healy, retired medical secretary, Herts, UK

In The Boarder, *Sue Hampton captures the emotion of loss that resonates with all of us who have lost someone we adore. When the time limits of grief are imposed on the main character, she searches for unanswered questions in improbable places. A chance meeting and short-lived bond help her find resolution. Beautifully written.*

Deeann Callis Graham, author*, US

A story of grief, remorse, revelation and resolution that had me riveted with finely & sympathetically drawn characters. A short story should grab the reader's attention from the outset; this one clutches the heart.

Virginia Moodie, social worker, Herts, UK

I found The Boarder *very moving and the relationship that develops between the two characters is deep and believable. I love the unpredictable ending, and the lines about 'the butterfly thing': 'The soul of the departed, landing a step ahead of me on the path, and then on a hedge so close I could have touched it. And jewelled of course. A last goodbye before it flies.' Beautiful healing words.*

Katherine Lunn, librarian, Cecil Jones Academy, Southend, Essex, UK

A poignant story, sensitively told, about the process of mourning and the comfort of sharing it.

Yan Christensen, Graham Greene Birthplace Trust, Berkhamsted, UK

I loved this account of a woman mourning her father. I found the prose lyrical and I enjoyed the way that information about the relationships between the mourner and her father, her partner and son were fed into the narrative by anecdote.

Christopher Walker-Lyne, social worker, York, UK

An insightful and evocative tale which manages to explore the raw pain of grief with a twist. Intriguing to the end; Sue Hampton writes with sensitivity ensuring she tells both sides of the story.

Claire Bavister, librarian, Flitwick, UK

This story takes the reader on an atmospheric journey through grief and loss, with a twist. Kate is haunted by the memories of her late father when she meets, by accident, someone who was at boarding school with him. A compelling read.

Deborah Bromley, Northants, UK

The Boarder

Steve could probably tell from the set of her shoulders at the screen.

"No reply from the boarding school?"

Kate shook her head, hoping he wouldn't ask her again why she didn't just phone, when the answer was so obvious. Because words like "possible", "visit" and "convenient time" would make way for the child who needed to see, to know – or else she'd cry.

"It'll have changed," she heard Steve say as he made for the kettle. "It's not as if they'll have … you know, a plaque in the dorm where his bed used to be." Kate looked up from the laptop at the kitchen table to the back of her husband's head, his hair straggling damp from the shower. Was that impatience talking? Irritation? Her friend Jayne had suggested the other day that Steve might even be jealous: "Because your grief occupies you." "Consumes, you mean?" she'd answered, and the smile had trailed more tears.

She accepted Steve's offer of more coffee and clicked off the email. She had no fresh words to explain what he couldn't process – this longing to track down the missing chapters in the narrative and find her father again, the boy who'd gone missing. Before the patient in Intensive Care, the wild, full-steam grandpa and the daddy who wrote poetry in a deckchair once the lawn was cut, his fingernails tipped with green.

"If it wasn't such a long drive," Steve broke in, "I'd say let's just go. Turn up. Refuse to leave."

Kate smiled. He could do that: the twist from critic to champion. Maybe he read her hurt better than she knew. Maybe the belief she'd lived with all her life, that her dad understood her best, most instinctively and unconditionally, wasn't fair on anyone else.

"Enough," she said, attempting a shrug. "It was a mad idea. Kind of grabbing in the dark."

A different kind of smile meant Steve remembered grabbing of a different kind, in the early hours, when she'd not only allowed it at last

11

but given him everything: all those feelings labels couldn't match. Holding on to everything snatched and out of reach, and trying to love.

Should she be apologising? At thirty-eight days of mourning, did he consider her over the limit now? Kate fetched a small plate to cover her coffee.

"I'm going for a walk," she said, turning towards the door. "Just a quick glass of air." It was her father's phrase; her thoughts were peppered with them.

"Take your phone," she heard on the doormat, but it was silent by the bed.

On the street, everything was as muted as seven forty-five on a Sunday should be, but the breeze felt far from balmy. Steve would be appalled if he knew she had no coat. Maybe he was watching her from the window, wondering whether to mention counselling again. Kate quickened her step. "Full speed ahead!" her dad used to say on a British beach, facing waves like pewter. And she'd push through them, gasping, to reach him.

Overhead, a red kite circled. Could their wingspan really be six foot? He'd know. Birds, flowers, trees … It made him sad towards the end when he couldn't retrieve the Latin labels he'd known for seventy years.

His camel mac! It was! She kept walking, faster now, because the man across the road, on the path through the park they called Butts Meadow, wasn't doddery but purposeful. The mac looked just as pale and loose around the same kind of frame – thin, a slight forward stoop of the shoulders. She saw the same awareness of the skies as he lifted his head, probably admiring the kite in flight. He was turning, like her father, to take in the flowers as he looked towards the bushes or the gardens backing on to the field – not just trying to name them but loving them too, grateful for them being there. So like him, it could be his twin. His ghost. Daddy.

She had to see his face. Opening her mouth as she began to run, she stopped short of calling. What, exactly? 'Wait!'? She could almost feel Steve's arm restrain her. But he wasn't here, and an old man just like her father was a couple of hundred metres away, no more.

The road that led to the high street suddenly offered up a stream of traffic to stop her crossing. On the other side the man in the mac was hidden a moment behind a family with a double buggy and a couple of kids meandering ahead, shouting. And another car … and she hadn't even pressed the button yet! Looking to the light, still red, she was ready to run anyway when she scanned the park and found he'd gone.

O.K., she told herself. Breathe. Think. Live. It was what her father would tell her. The man had turned into the allotments, or down the alley that led to the high street via the school. Perhaps through a gate into his own back garden. Or maybe he was heading for an early service at the church, like her dad as a schoolboy in chapel, before he lost faith in everything but light and shadow, and love, and her.

"See," she could imagine him saying. "I haven't left you. I'm just round the corner, that's all." Without bothering to halt the tear that slid down one cheek, Kate crossed the road. There was still air worth drinking and she'd forgotten to shiver.

"You didn't tell Steve?" checked Jayne the next Saturday morning, in the new café that collected for refugees.

"He thinks I'm going crazy as it is."

"So have you been looking out for this old man ever since?"

"Why do you think I wanted the seat facing the street?"

"I guess I might do the same," said Jayne, taking off her running cap. Kate had no idea how she could look so sleek and fresh after a session in the gym.

"*You*'d have caught him before he disappeared!"

"He wasn't an apparition," Jayne pointed out, and stirred her *flat white* in a way that seemed measured, therapist-style. "And I'd do the cognitive thing too."

People didn't seem to expect the cognitive of Kate. She assured Jayne she'd told herself repeatedly that any chase or search would be pointless, lead only to disappointment and delay the healing process.

Jayne nodded. "Tell yourself one last time."

In the dream she pushed her way through dripping branches in a forest hammered by rain and rattled by wind, the beige mac lost, found and lost again but always crisscrossed by trees. Crying out, she woke to find Steve was already up. She looked at the time: almost a quarter to eight. Maybe her father's doppelganger was a creature of routines. She pulled on jeggings and a sweater and trod lightly on the stairs in spite of the TV she could hear from the lounge. A minute later she was crossing at the lights and walking down the path to the park – where she tried not to feel intimidated by a dog straining at the lead to bark frenetically in her face.

"He's harmless, honestly," said the owner, a straggle of a woman.

"Sure!"

This had to stop. It couldn't be normal. Sweat, fear, imaginings. Kate looked up, hoping for a red kite to take her soaring but still. Above the dewy field, only crows and pigeons hurried in their different directions but a dark cloud drew steadily towards her. Laughing inwardly at the way everything had become personal now, even the weather, as if the world outside her window was just a metaphor for her own small, predictable grief, Kate looked back to the road. And there he was, approaching with an eye on the same cloud. The wrong eyes. Even though a short-sighted drunk might be fooled by the shape of the face, and the soft, streaky grey of the hair, they weren't her father's.

She realised she had looked a moment or two too long. There was a question now in the way he looked back.

"Are you all right?" he asked.

"Yes, I'm fine."

"There's a bench over there, if you need to sit down."

Kate suspected she must look like Rochester's wife, and smell worse. Otherwise she might have sat and hoped he'd join her, so she could tell him he was very like her father; that was all. Because he looked like a good listener.

And she was still looking, hesitating, when he said, "You're sad, my dear. I'm sorry."

Her smile fell away. But she thanked him and said she'd head back before the rain, waving a hand to show him how close home was.

"Good idea," he said. "I fear it's going to bucket down." Words her dad would have said, and so nearly the way he would have said them.

Smiling, Kate said goodbye. Nothing had broken. All she felt was warmth, until the first rain chased her to the front door.

When she told Steve a few minutes later, she guessed he was relieved. Fantasy over; the real world striking back. She appreciated the hug but as

14

far as the real world went, she wasn't sure what difference it could make.

"You missed Jamie," he said as she withdrew.

Kate stared. After a fortnight of travelling as if he'd broken up with technology as well as Livi Andrews, their boy had called – at a time when normally he'd be sure to catch her. Under questioning, Steve said he was fine, liking Malaysia, moving on in a few days. Eating? Yes, he imagined so. Sleeping? Well, now and then.

"He asked about you."

Of course he did, bless him. "Don't tell me what you said."

A couple of days later Kate was in the supermarket when she glimpsed the camel mac at the far end of the aisle. She caught him at the bakery end, putting on his glasses to read labels.

"Hello again," she said, from behind. Feeling glad, when he turned, of her lipstick, perfume and just-washed hair – of being assembled, at least on the outside – she smiled. "I don't know your name. I'm Kate." She glanced towards the café area. "Can I buy you a coffee?"

"Kate," he said, and held out his hand. His grip as he shook hers was light and cool. "I'm glad to see you looking well. I'm Anthony, and thank you. That would be lovely."

When she invited him to buy his bread first he said he just liked to inhale, and she agreed as they walked that coffee was good for that too, but lily of the valley was best of all. At one of the little tables for two, he took off the mac to reveal a chocolate brown V-neck pullover that might have been a Christmas present, a crisp cream collar and a red tie. He was dapper. Not something her dad ever aspired to be.

"On Sunday," she began, and he looked up, waiting, from his cappuccino. Explaining about the mistake, she ducked the d-words she only used in her head and talked about 'losing' him.

"You thought you'd found him," said Anthony, and touched her hand on the table a moment. "I'm sorry. I did the butterfly thing, when my wife died."

"The butterfly thing?"

"The soul of the departed, landing a step ahead of me on the path, and then on a hedge so close I could have touched it. And jewelled of course. A last goodbye before it flies."

"Psyche," she remembered. "That's beautiful."

She had to ask about his wife because she could see he wanted to tell her.

"She was too good for me, and I don't mean class. Just too good. I was a slow learner but living with her made me a better person in the end." He drank, and she didn't mention the chocolate on his top lip. "Would you like to tell me about your father?" he asked. "Because we can talk about the Ancient Greeks if you prefer."

Kate said that would be a one-sided conversation. But how to begin? With the end? Not without making a public spectacle. She mentioned the poetry and the gardening, the galleries and concerts, walks and talks. Omitting the feel, when she linked her arm in his, of the worn old mac beneath her fingers, and the line of his bone under the warm skin. Anthony nodded a little, and asked about her mother, so she gave him the short version: "She left Dad for a neighbour when I was at university, and Dad said these things happened. No blame." She looked around the café and away, like a reflex, from two faces she knew. "That was my role. The pair of them had to die in a car crash before I really forgave them."

Then, as he said that was very understandable and her father must have been a remarkable man, she remembered. "I was on my way to find a frame for this," she said, and pulled out the black-and-white photograph in its A4 wallet. She handed it to Anthony. "Second in from the left, front row. You know the way people who fought in the war wouldn't talk about it? With Dad it was boarding school." She hated to imagine the little boy crying in the dormitory so no one could hear. "I never saw this photo. He must have been so unhappy."

Anthony's face had reshaped. He'd found his glasses now and his mouth was open.

"This is my school," he said. "I knew him."

That evening, when she told him, Steve looked as if she'd reported an encounter with the Velveteen Rabbit. She had to remind him of the time he crossed a New York street to avoid his ex-boss from Luton days. No, she explained, Anthony Garrod wasn't actually in the House photo because he was in Hannibal, not Aristotle, and two years ahead – although Steve really wouldn't think so, if he saw him, to look at him now. But he was there, and she didn't need to bother the snotty place now because Anthony had taken her back, with his memories, to the way it was. In words close to Anthony's she passed on Matron almost too wide for the doorway; the shell-shocked Latin teacher prone to tears over Horace; the way once a month the hall became a cinema to show stiff, heroic films that broke down and shot off a tangle of reel. Thick blue writing paper piled for Sunday evening letters while rabbits emerged on the manicured grass at dusk. The velvety red chair that cushioned his buttocks when he sat outside the Headmaster's office preparing them for the cane. "Not Dad," she said. "Anthony. He reckons he was a show-off himself. That was why he liked school, for the audience."

She'd tell Steve some other time that he recalled her father's shyness and sensitivity, and the jeers afterwards when a teacher delivered a poem he'd written. Poor Anthony had known he'd said too much, and apologised again, but she realised she'd known anyway. Her father had been a soft target, a lonely, homesick boy who tried to delete everything afterwards but the hills and the river.

Steve kept saying it was incredible until she told him she hadn't made it up, "for crying out loud" – and wished she could do exactly that. Leaving him in the kitchen, she sat on the sofa and looked at the photograph she'd displayed beside the TV. Her father's eight-year-old frame was slight inside the oversized uniform, and whatever the boys had been instructed to chorus for the camera, there was no smile in his eyes.

"I love you, Dad," she told him in her head.

Over the next few weeks she met Anthony four times. He escorted her around his allotment, where the marrows and courgettes were fat and gleaming and he told her proudly what a show the hollyhocks would make, come summer. It was a bit more of a struggle than it used to be, he admitted, so she offered to help. But before she had the chance, he arrived at the park bench with a basket full of the freshest food she'd ever seen, apologising for the traces of mud he'd missed. She told him "sorry" was banned and he said he'd try.

There was another coffee, this time at the café in a bookshop where he greeted her with freesias in damp tissue and an elastic band – "No lily of the valley but I'll keep my eyes peeled." Holding them, she pointed out a few of the poets her dad revered on the shelves. Too clever, Anthony said, for him. Too modern.

Then on a warmer, bluer day they walked along the canal and, watching his camel sleeve swing at arm's reach, she asked him if there was anything else he could tell her about her father.

"I didn't know him well, Kate. I wish I had. I'm sorry."

For a while they just took in the sunlight, the moorhens and swans, the breeze and the narrowboats in easy silence. Then the shattered reflections of leaves on the water prompted her to tell him her father's last holiday was really for Monet, near Giverny, where he'd longed to go for seventy years. And where he found he'd left his camera in the B and B. "He hoped he could hold on to the pictures in his head," she said. "I like to think they were still there at the end."

She explained how she'd planned to go with him but let him down, but Anthony stopped her.

"Your dad was right," he said. "No blame, remember."

When the canal led them into town again he asked her, as they parted, whether she'd like to go to his house for tea one day. "A bit of a box really. I'm in sheltered accommodation, much too fancy but it saves the children worry. Dicky heart. I hear you can make chocolate cake with beetroot and mine's coming along nicely."

She didn't have her diary and he couldn't quite recall his new phone number, so she said she'd see him on Sunday morning and bring it then. On an impulse she kissed his cheek, struck by its chill softness, and he squeezed her hand.

It was easier to tell Steve a basic minimum, and as brightly as possible. And to make excuses with Jayne, who knew the terms Steve didn't actually use. Dependency. Transference. They'd all think she needed to move on – without suggesting where or how – and Anthony only took her back. Because angels were not in their vocabularies.

But she hadn't expected it from Jamie. He rang again that Sunday, just as she was watching the clock with a camel coat in mind. Not much to report from somewhere called Shah Alam except a plan to go "off-route" that wasn't meant to scare her. "All good," he said, and then, a blink later, "Tell me about this old man then." Like a suspicious cop.

She explained but he interrupted, reminding her of the time he'd had that trouble online and the school didn't take it seriously but his grandad helped. The line was bad. She heard snatches: "humiliating ritual stuff" and "compass points in the arm ..." For a moment she held the phone away, but when she pulled it back she thought she made out "a nappy for a mummy's boy". "Jamie!" she yelled. "Why are you telling me this? Enough."

She could tell he was crying, in some concrete city where dead animals roasted in the street, for the schoolboy and the grandfather who understood. Kate was crying too. She tried to tell him she'd got the message and she wouldn't dig up more than she could bear but somehow, Anthony helped.

"Jamie," she said, "I love you." But the line was dead.

The clock said ten to eight. He might ring back. But she couldn't let Anthony down. The park was full of small footballers and their dads, and she remembered Anthony was rugger captain and opening bat – unlike her father, who was always last on the team. She sat on the bench a while, trying not to think. She checked her watch, and ventured up to the allotments. No camel coat. No purposeful walk with stoop. Had she missed him? Perhaps he'd forgotten, or overslept. After almost half an hour she went home.

All week she kept an eye out for him, in the supermarket, on the high street, along the canal. Over the gate to the allotments she watched the figures with their gloves, kneeling pads and wheelbarrows early each afternoon, but he wasn't one of them.

By the time Friday came, bringing the sunshine back, she'd convinced herself that whatever else had come up, this was the day he'd be checking on the butternut squash. But amongst the women the only man was stocky and bearded, a smoker in a Paddington hat. Opening the gate this time, and heading towards the hat, Kate heard a voice telling her the angel had flown on to the next lost soul grieving in search of butterflies. The sort of thing her father would say, with a smile close to a wink.

But maybe it was more a case of reality biting back again and warning her off. From a radio, probably a small one on a potting shed shelf, she heard something more robust: a song Jamie used to play in his room not so long ago. *Let it go.*

She stopped, and would have turned away but the music cut and someone was calling her.

"Hello? Miss? You looking for Anthony?"

The smoker had peeled off his hat. His hair was flat and damp. Her dad would call his cheeks ruddy.

"Yes," she said. "I'm a friend."

19

"We all are … He's gone. Heart attack." Behind her a woman planted a spade and watched them.

"Oh, no …" Kate was shaking.

"He was a proper gentleman, not like that Eton mob. Did you know him long?"

She shook her head. The man said that was all he could tell her but if she wrote her number down he'd let her know about the funeral. It took a while for her to find a scrap of paper and a biro that worked against the top of the gate where the grain was less than smooth. Looking up she saw a flurry of butterflies, but not one came close. She thanked him, and walked back along the path, through the park to the traffic lights.

It was over then. But why? What for?

Steve held her when she told him, and told her things didn't need reasons.

"Yes," she said. "Sometimes it's enough to glimpse someone. A good human."

"I'm hugging one," he said. "You gave as much as he did."

She supposed he meant time. But she wished she could hold on to that, squeeze it, eke it out like people did with everything, post-war. Or hold the arm in the camel sleeve instead, one more time. It didn't seem to matter anymore which of them wore it.

"Don't go to the funeral," Steve murmured.

He was afraid for her, she knew that. Too soon, too much. He wouldn't be there on one side to help her stand, with Jamie tall and quiet on the other. And they were right, all of them. This time she'd listen.

The church was out of town, the one he attended with the wife who made him a better man. At the crematorium his ashes would be buried with hers, his allotment friends said. Did she need a lift there? No, she'd thanked them. She couldn't …

Kate pulled on the same black dress; it was the only one she had. But there was no rain-beaten mud to splash her legs this time, and she slipped in at the back, like the acquaintance she was, watching the coffin carried in, and telling herself there was no camel coat inside. Listening to the bio, she felt disconnected from the successful businessman, the golf club, sailing holidays, Round Table. The Anthony she knew seemed strangely missing until "the loss of his beloved wife". She hadn't expected 1, Corinthians, and couldn't have read the last verse the way his daughter did from the pulpit, her slightly antipodean voice only fracturing on the love word that was always quickest to break. Introducing *The Day thou Gavest, Lord has ended*, the Rector explained that like all the boys at his boarding school, Anthony knew hundreds of hymns off by heart but this one was sung each Sunday at Evensong and had been a favourite ever since.

Kate resisted the desire to vanish as the organ began. Instead she stood and sang a little. After the final prayer, as the crowd moved slowly towards the door, she kept her eyes on the stone floor, only lifting them to the light outside. The allotment crew being waylaid by Anthony's daughter would think her rude, but she needed air without words.

The sun felt brand new. It pricked the tears free.

"Excuse me!"

She turned, glanced around, turned back. His daughter's eyes, blue like his, held hers. She was more or less Kate's age but fuller, smarter and holding together better.

"Kate Judd?"

"Yes?"

"I'm Ruth Garrod. Thank you for coming. Daddy mentioned you last time I called." She opened her handbag. Kate waited. "Sorry, it's in here somewhere."

Puzzled, Kate stood, unable to guess. Anthony's daughter produced an envelope. Kate read her name in writing that might have been a five year old's. Or an old man's once the heart tightened.

"Thank you," she said. "He knew my father."

But now the blue eyes had let her go. The hostess was wanted; Kate remembered that well. Apologising, Ruth Garrod said she hoped Kate would join them for refreshments, and was gone.

Taking the envelope to the edge of the churchyard, she had – still minus sunglasses – to find some shade under a eucalyptus tree. She pulled out a folded piece of lined paper, the kind he'd held as a shopping list in the supermarket.

There were only three words, in the same shaky print.

Bully. Forgive me.

And a kiss.

Away for Christmas *shows just how constructive the generation gap can prove to be at times. A lonely and pedantic old lady meets her match in an incurably cheerful and easy-going young driver who manages to break through her tough veneer and glimpse into her real self. How they infuse each other with new life is what makes this dialogue and character-driven Christmas story a heart-warming tale of humanity.*

Lata Tokhi, blogger/web publisher, India

A new friendship, a new perspective, a different Christmas. This is a festive tale where a chance meeting changes the status quo, not only for the main protagonists, but for the bystanders as well. I loved the colloquialisms in the dialogue. Away for Christmas *is* Driving Miss Daisy *for the digital age. This is an engaging story where the characters' quips make you smile.*

Elaine Marsh, education support, Yorkshire, UK

Away for Christmas *is a heart-warming story of young and old. Sue Hampton really brings her characters to life and draws the reader into their world brilliantly.*

Heather Pretty, ex-school librarian, Northants, UK

Sue Hampton's cleverly written characters are a pleasure to spend time with and the twists in her story make for a fuzzy feeling of festiveness.

Elizabeth Parikh, teacher, Bedfordshire, UK

As always Sue Hampton grabs the attention of her audience ... and makes us think.

Emma Skipper, PA, Burton-upon-Trent, UK

Away for Christmas *is a lovely short story. Full of hope and the true meaning of Christmas, it put a smile on my face.*

Lorna Rowntree-O'Donnell, Flitwick, Bedfordshire, UK

Away for Christmas

"But he's never late," Gerry repeated.

It was all very well for Mel to keep saying he'd be there soon but how the Dickens did *she* know?

"Bye-ee," she interrupted her, and put down the phone, forgetting the Merry Christmas bit. But Mel already had her present, nicely wrapped: a reward. This taxi palaver was different. She was a paying customer, a loyal one.

Gerry sat by the window in her best coat and purple beret, watching the rain batter the puddles below. Her stick lay across the sill and her suitcase stood upright on its little wheels beside her. Where in Hades was he?

The car had changed a few times over the years but the arrangements never did. It wasn't as if there was snow this time to throw the country into disarray. After twenty-odd Christmases, Gerry would have thought he could time it to the second, bar Hell or high water or asteroid attack.

She was examining the old bay tree – in case she'd only watered it in her head – when the sound of an engine made her look down again. A man stepped out of the car but the body shape wasn't right. She grabbed the stick and waved it.

"No, no!" she called. "Wrong company!"

She saw the man pushing the doors at the bottom and heading for the stairs. Agitated, she made her way to her door, but he was ringing her bell before she'd reached it, just the way she wished people wouldn't. She'd told Mel the next person to rattle her letterbox might get his mouth stopped with a walking stick.

She opened, leaving the chain on. He was a whippersnapper.

"Mrs Chalmers?"

Good hair, but much too much of it for anyone with no bosom. "Where's the other one?"

"Roy died," said the boy. "Set off on a job yesterday and never finished

RAVELLED & OTHER STORIES

it. They found him in the car park, kind of peaceful. I'm Kyle."

"Died?" cried Gerry. She felt the heat in her cheeks as the sweat surfaced above her top lip. "Lord save us. So that's his name, Roy. Of course it is. What am I like? Dead?"

"You look alive and kicking to me."

Roy never talked to her like that. No respect. No one said no to young people and they were far too familiar. Except the ones with hoods, smoking on the street, swaggering around with their trousers half-down.

"I'll kick *you* in a minute," she muttered to herself, and pulled the door to.

This one had no proper uniform. His jacket wasn't even buttoned up and he wore no tie. Let him wait. Let him think. People needed to think more. It was a shock.

Gerry made rumbling noises in her throat as she trudged back to the window to collect her case. She'd forgotten her stick so she had to lean and grab the table, then the chair and the corner of the bookcase. Some books fell and made her jump. A squeal escaped. What was she doing?

"You all right in there?" she heard, and before she could tell him she was perfectly fine he was in her flat, standing there in her hallway, looking around into the lounge.

"What are you, a cat burglar?"

"Only in my spare time. You didn't shut the door," he told her. "I thought you might need some help."

"*Well I don't*," she usually said, going down the steps into the charity shop or making her way out to the front of the church for Communion. Then she'd tell Mel, "*I shouldn't be rude, should I?*" Roy always carried her case. It was what she paid for. Not all this bother. Had she packed her tablets?

The boy handed her the stick and picked up her case, angling out an elbow for her to take. She ignored it and followed him, looking at the hair below his collar and wondering why his mother didn't take some scissors to it.

"You always go away for Christmas, do you?"

"I might do. Carl, you say your name is? Have you got a surname?"

"Kyle Green."

"Sounds like a bus stop!"

That left him laughing. At the door she glanced into the kitchen. No red lights. Fridge door properly shut. She pulled a used envelope out of her pocket. "I'm just checking," she said. "You need lists. That's where young people go wrong."

"My phone tells me stuff." He pulled it out.

"No substitute for thinking," Gerry told him. "It's good for the brain."

She pushed past him to grab the rail and lead the way down. Roy died! She hadn't seen that coming. She might have reconsidered.

He stepped ahead of her at the double doors and held one open for her, then told her, "Hang on," and did the same with the car.

Cars were getting trickier. Gerry managed, but her breathing was high in her chest and the seatbelt kept dodging her.

"Let me," he said, and clicked her in.

Young people always had to make out everything was a doddle, a piece of cake. But she didn't suppose he'd know where the Chancellor of the Exchequer went to school. She didn't suppose he could spell Exchequer.

"Excelsior Hotel," she said, as he started the engine. "Barnes Street. Do you know the way or do you have to ask your phone?"

"Sat nav," he said, pointing to a small screen. "We'll be fine." He started to back out of the drive. "Looking forward to Christmas, then?"

If she had the kind of Christmas she could look forward to, she wouldn't book a week in a London hotel, would she? Not many people knew, apart from Mr Singh at the paper shop. Just Mel, because she'd got Thursday off for good behaviour. A holiday was an excuse to tidy the place. One collected so much gubbins, and clear-outs were good for morale.

But letters were letters and she'd never left the flat before knowing that they weren't in it somewhere.

The boy at the wheel started to make jokes about inflatable Santas. "Take a break now," she told him. "No need to chat all the way. I don't pay for that, just a smooth ride."

"You want me to shut up?"

"Just drive me, Kyle Green," she told him. "That's your job."

"Certainly," he said, and in the mirror Gerry saw him smile to himself

26

as he added, "madam."

It was what her father used to call her, even when she was four or five – a fat child with hair that liked to sprout. They were indoor memories but outside it was India. There was a maid who teased her with the broom, chasing her feet with it to make her laugh as she jumped because her laugh was even bigger than her appetite.

Just for the sound of it she laughed, and tried to picture her father, before the hospital business and all that hoo-hah with lawyers, as a young dad with a daughter to tease. She thought she might as well get rid of the old photos too. Daddy didn't think her Scotsman was good enough but he could have kept his oar out. People should.

"I'm a survivor," she said.

"I can see that," said Kyle.

"It's not as easy as it looks."

A female voice cut in uninvited.

"Who the Dickens is that?" she asked, as Kyle turned right as instructed. "Is your girlfriend hiding in the boot?"

"That's just the sat nav," he said, pointing to the screen. "I'll put it on mute."

"Put it on dumb," said Gerry, and laughed. "Does it email too? The woman on the BBC told me to email about the birds and there was one in the bush yesterday, a waggle tail job. The trouble with the television people is they don't seem to understand that not everyone has a computer to tell them to turn right. We have to think for ourselves, and pay through the ear for postage stamps."

"That's where all my money goes, then. It leaks out of my ears. Could explain a lot."

"Ha!" cried Gerry.

But what should she have said? Body parts got muddled sometimes. Phrases she'd been using all her life had bits missing, like the Christmas decorations.

She watched him adjusting the screen.

"I got rid of my car in the end. No point in turning mouldy as Stilton if no one wants to eat you. Young people don't appreciate the legs they have. Mine lost the hang of it. I have to talk them round."

"I bet you're good at that," said Kyle, eyes on the road.

"I am! I'm like a sat nav!" cried Gerry. "But not as bossy!"

"You can be as bossy as you like, Mrs Chalmers. You're paying."

Gerry's chest rose. Heavens to Betsy, how many times a year did she have to tell people?

"I never married! I didn't get asked! And who says I would have said yes anyway? Men will take liberties if you don't lay down the gauntlet."

"My mum never married either," said Kyle.

She told him she was sorry to hear that. People had no idea of the basics nowadays but strictly speaking it wasn't his fault. She tugged open her bag of toffees and began to suck one.

"Do you always stay in the same hotel?"

"Why shouldn't I? They keep the room for me. People overlook the importance of bearings."

Around them the noise was gathering: rain on metal, the rush of tyres through water that swished and sprayed. But Kyle Green was like a boy in an armchair with a *neeyow*, moving out and overtaking a dirty white van.

"Steady on, James Bond. Does the car become a speedboat or are we going to fly?"

"I'm at your service," he said. "Which would you prefer?"

"If you're going to answer back, save it for her," she told him, waving a hand at the sat nav. "She's got no stick."

He'd be better off in a go-kart on a disused runway. But she busied herself with unwrapping toffees, sucking as squelchily as she liked and picking strings from her teeth. Soon she recognized Finchley. She liked to see Jewish men in black, showing respect, walking together respectably with their little caps and hair. Traditions should be upheld. People didn't understand today. Kyle Green didn't, with his gum and his cheek, and she might have to complain to his superiors.

Soon the car was held up in a queue as vehicles lined up from all directions. They were surrounded, just like Custer at the Battle of Little Big Horn.

"What the Dickens?" she cried, because a man was in the road, looking at them, no spear but a bucket. She didn't like his face. "Sitting target!"

Now he was advancing. Gerry grabbed the edge of her seat, knuckles tight.

"No, no, no! Daddy!"

"You're all right, Miss Chalmers."

With her hands on the sides of her head, Gerry squinted through the glass ahead. Kyle Green signalled to the man, who ambled right in front of the car. Gerry saw flowers in the bucket. She peeled her hands away and told herself to breathe.

Kyle Green wound down the window on his side and gave the man a few coins from his trouser pocket and a "Happy Christmas, mate." As the man nodded his head and put his hands together, Kyle Green handed her a bunch of red roses in cellophane.

"There you go. You can ask for a vase in your room."

The cellophane was wet and dripped onto her bare leg.

"You can't sleep with flowers in your room," she told him. "Carbon dioxide. You wake up dead."

He grinned. "But you're a survivor."

"No scent," she said, sniffing.

"So," he said, tucking the flowers out of the way, "what do you do there?"

"What?"

"In the hotel, I mean …"

"I clean the toilets! I won't be interrogated! What do you think? I stay there. I sleep in the bed and eat in the restaurant."

"Sounds like a nice rest," said Kyle. "But you could spice it up this year and sleep in the restaurant and eat in the bed."

He wasn't looking at her but Gerry thought he was amused. Suddenly she pictured herself with waiters on each side of the bed, serving her Christmas dinner.

"Ha!" she cried. "I might give it a try. What about you?"

"Me?"

"What do you do at Christmas, Kyle Green? Drink beer and watch *EastEnders*?"

"You know me so well, Miss Chalmers."

"I don't," she objected. "We're not acquainted. I've seen the way people go on outside the coffee shops, kissing people's cheeks as if they want to have their babies."

"Yeah, my sister's like that."

"My sister isn't. She's dead, so her kiss might be on the chilly side." Gerry laughed wildly. "Heavens to betsy, I'm terrible. You're a bad influence on me with your beer and your unmarried mother. I expect you eat off a tray in front of the television."

"No," he said. "From the pizza box."

He grinned and she wondered whether he was teasing again.

"Pizza!" she scoffed. "I don't suppose you'd know a sprout if it hit you in the eye."

"Not while I'm driving, Miss Chalmers, if you don't mind."

"Ha!" She told herself she must be more dignified. How did sprouts start flying around the place? It was all out of control and that was his fault. Her cousin used to do the same and then she'd be the one who earned a spanking.

She adjusted herself in the passenger seat but her ankles still felt heavy. He was so light and quick the way he changed gears, looked in the mirrors and pressed on the brakes, as if he didn't have to think about anything. He probably hadn't thought since he turned the key in the ignition; young people didn't, and this one had no father.

"Mine used to strap me," she said. "No mollycoddling. Some of the parents at the school were soft. Didn't dare say boo to their little goslings. Dad went for my bare legs. I'd try to sneak in but he'd jump out at me with his belt. Made a point, you know."

"It's the wrong point."

Startled, Gerry frowned in his direction. Wrong? Who said?

"Pardon me?" she asked. His eyes were on the traffic queue ahead. "I didn't quite catch."

"I don't agree with parents hitting children."

"No, no, no, not hitting, just a bit of a swipe …"

"If you ask me, children need love, not violence."

"They need lines in the sand. That's what's lacking. There's no moral fibre without it. I didn't ask you, in fact. You wait till you've lived a bit.

30

You'll learn."

"I hope not."

Gerry breathed out long and hard. Drivers weren't meant to cross swords like Errol Flynn. He knew nothing, with his bossy sat nav and his girl's hair and his silly jokes about sprouts in bed.

"I've asked you before," she told him, her cheeks reddening and the moisture above her mouth starting to bead. "I have blood pressure. If I want a debate I'll go to the House of Commons. Let's keep it sweet, shall we?"

"Absolutely, madam."

Was he chewing gum? He adjusted the screen again and Gerry flinched as Bossyboots came back, with orders to turn left at the roundabout ahead when she could have told him that herself.

"You can't help being a pipsqueak but I've lived a whole life," she told him.

"I bet," he said. "I'd like to hear about your life."

She could have retorted that he hadn't liked hearing about her dad and his belt. "You'll have to let me think," she said. "I'm not used to this. Roy and I talked cricket and a bit of rugger. I've no plans for an autobiography. Do you know how old I am?"

"More than seventy?"

"I'm eighty-two. That's a lot of living."

"Wow."

"Not so wow lately. I can't go out on my own, you see, so church bods like good old Mel escort me. It's a question of falling. Leaves and rain, ice and slopes. Mel made me mince pies and I had them for breakfast, two every day. But I used to drive and fly and run things. Lists, that's the secret. Cross off. Get through. Job done."

Gerry felt tired. It was all a bit much. One dead chauffeur and another who bought her red roses from a man who might have mugged the pair of them. But she used to be reckless once, when her knees were made of rubber and she could dance the night away.

"Not everyone wants jibber jabber and the frumious bandersnatch, with *Keep left* from She Who Must Be Obeyed," she muttered at the window.

"Understood," he said.

She closed her eyes but it was impossible to relax with rain beating like a war dance. At this rate she'd be going straight to bed in Room 23. She remembered the days when she used to take the stairs and carry her own case just to show them.

"What did you run?" he asked.

What? He was like a spider that kept coming back up the plughole.

"Run? The Marathon. The hundred metres. The hop, skip and diddle. Ha!" Gerry laughed so much that she spluttered a little.

Kyle offered her a bottle of water that stood by the gear stick but she batted it away.

"I ran wild. So he sent me to boarding school, and I went a bit wilder. On the roof. I monkeyed up and dangled a brassiere around the old weathercock – black lace, extra-large. They were going to expel me. Daddy pointed out the humour they'd missed. Overlooked it. Such a fuss. Ha!"

She told him about the gust of wind that gave her the habdabs and almost sent the bra flying off the mast.

"It was a different kind of era," she said. "Nowadays the teachers hang out of see-through blouses."

"I must have gone to the wrong school," said Kyle.

Gerry coughed, reached for the water bottle and wiped the rim on her sleeve. She wished her face wouldn't go so red in front of people.

"I'd better stop," she told him, using her hand to clear the water from her chin. "If you're going to be naughtier than me we'll be in a pickle before long. I'm a bad influence. The headmistress told my father. But brassieres don't hurt people."

"Oh, I don't know," said Kyle. "They might if they flew through the air at speed and whacked you between the eyes. Underwired! Ouch!"

"You've no business knowing so much about ladies' underwear, Kyle Green. Keep driving."

Martin Hedges supposed he'd better prepare the newer members of staff for Miss Geraldine Chalmers. With her enormous red hands and her straight-down bulk that looked set for a scrum, she was more of a spectacle than she used to be. These days her straggly hair was whiter than chicken breast and looked just as greasy. But she still had a wink straight out of a cartoon, and a chesty laugh that alcohol could turn into a roar.

Over the years he'd made notes from the snippets she'd offered, so he could show her the following Christmas that he cared enough to remember. But he still couldn't fit it all together in any kind of sequence, and the truth was she'd become less and less coherent. Context had gone and anecdotes were thrown out randomly, with no thread to connect them. He wasn't sure she took much notice of anyone who happened to be in earshot, least of all him.

Who knew what she might say at the sight of an Asian face at breakfast? Sanjay was a good lad and he wouldn't want him taking offence or registering a complaint along the lines of racism. And young Toyah might struggle to hold back four-letter words if told she needed elocution lessons or advised to buy a skirt that left more to the imagination.

"So she's crazy?" deduced Toyah, grimacing grimly.

"Hm." Martin rather liked the look of Toyah's singing gran, who'd be stepping into the breach for the Christmas Day cabaret. He'd checked her out online: Toyah's curves without the pout. But he didn't think Miss Chalmers would approve.

He explained about loud noises. A couple of years ago some pans clattered in the kitchens and she'd cowered with her hands on her head, whimpering, like a soldier in the trenches under mortar attack. He hinted at a growing tendency to sniper fire, with no warning and no apology.

"More than anything else she's lonely," he finished. For someone so loud and so vivid, she was shy too – didn't like to intrude on people who *had* people.

"I'm not surprised," said Toyah, and turned away.

When should he tell old Gerry, he wondered, that by next Christmas he'd have given all this up to collect his pension?

That morning he'd checked the notebook as a kind of revision.

Never married but asked once. Or nearly asked? Wanted to be asked? A Scot?

It wasn't the kind of thing one asked any guest, least of all Geraldine Chalmers. He remembered telling her three years ago about his divorce. "Jumping juniper!" she'd cried. "Is it an epidemic? Don't vows mean anything?" and when he'd chosen silence something must have penetrated, some awareness of the world as people live it, because she'd added, squeezing her napkin roll, "Commiserations. Unfortunate business. Plough on, that's my advice."

Has lived in India, Singapore, Germany. Doing what? Diplomatic service? Or was that her father?

He'd heard her use words like plebs, oiks and riffraff. No idea of political correctness whatsoever.

She liked to remember being naughty at boarding school. *Hockey and cricket team captain but can't swim. Not academic but prides self on common sense.*

He'd added a note to self: to avoid politics. *True Blue, teller at elections. Thatcher fan.*

Not a lady of leisure though. *Matron in a boys' boarding school? Talk of 'the san' and rugby injuries.*

Misses having a garden.

There were details of her favourite drinks, starters, mains and desserts, every one of them so English you'd think she'd never left the country.

Martin had been a young man when she'd first stayed at The Excelsior. But she wasn't the kind of older woman you flirted with, even delicately. No Mrs Robinson. She drank more then, enough to unsteady her even in her flat shoes, and she'd finish her evening meal with a cigar. "Christmas only," she told him. "Annual wickedness," she'd say, excited as a child, as if she'd played a successful prank. More than once other guests asked to be moved further away from her table, and he suspected it wasn't only the smoke that bothered them but the way she narrowed her eyes on the assembled company while she blew it between her thick lips. As if she was surveying the scene and finding those who peopled it at fault – or invisible.

Even then conversation didn't flow so much as spark and fade, race forward and hit the buffers. Now she was cut adrift in the world, not just from him but from everything, maybe even her own past. And it struck him that for all the weight she'd piled on, she'd shrunk.

Noticing that it was three thirty-five, Martin was considering calling the taxi company when a car pulled up outside and he heard her the moment the door opened.

"Aha! Down with the anchor. Into port!"

She was holding on to a young man who certainly wasn't Roy, and apparently enjoying it.

"Is it Hawaii?" the driver asked her, confidentially. "You'll need a grass skirt."

Since she was holding her stick with the arm that wasn't linked in his, she could only elbow him as she cried, "None of your cheek."

"Ouf!" the driver joked, as if she'd winded him.

"Martin Hedges!" she hailed him, lifting her stick at him like a sword. "Rescue me. This is what I've had to put up with all the way from the shires. Meet Kyle Green. He's not a bus stop. I would have got off."

She laughed, unaware as always that everyone in the foyer, bar and restaurant must have heard, looked, leaned, listened, wondered. Had she ever been so loud, so mad, so showy? The laugh rolled out longer than a queue at a Christmas checkout.

"No Roy?" he asked the driver.

"He died. I'm the new boy. Traffic was mental."

"That makes two of us," she cried, looking at the driver and winking. It was such a big, generous wink that it could have been meant for both of them and possibly Sanjay too, waiting to take her case.

Kyle Green had a bunch of roses in his free hand, their red heads down. He gave them to Martin and asked if he could find a vase. Silently Martin passed them to Sanjay.

"Give the boy a mince pie and some hot chocolate. Sit down with us. We'll have a party."

"I'm sorry, Gerry," said the driver, "I've got to head off, remember? But we'll keep in touch, yeah?"

Gerry?! On the old woman's face was a smile that was almost elastic. Martin hoped his own incredulity was properly masked. She'd been Miss Chalmers to him for thirty years.

Now Kyle Green had one hand on her arm and she wasn't swatting it, or screaming for her father.

"*Ja, mein herr.*" She patted her coat pocket. "A Christmas present from my chauffeur. Not just roses either."

"Enjoy! I'll see you on 27th."

"Make sure you do, Sonny Jim. Stay alive if you can."

"I will if you will. Happy Christmas! See ya."

"Toodle-oo to you-hoo."

Since Sanjay was dealing with the roses, Martin would have to carry the case himself. She waved one hand without turning as she hobbled towards the lift, and once in, felt inside the coat pocket.

"It's a mobile phone," she told him, holding it out like a ticket at a barrier. "It loops the loop and dances the fandango. They change them like underpants, young people. You can write letters on it, short ones without a stamp, and put zero for hug at the end. I've got the Sonny Jim's number. Ha!"

"I see," said Martin. "I hope you're well, Miss Chalmers."

"Of course I'm not. I'm a wreck and the marbles are all over the shop. Watch out!" She put the phone back in her pocket. "I've had a tutorial. Never too late for further education, my friend. I don't suppose Mrs Hedges came to her senses, like Hosea's wife?"

"I'm still divorced, Miss Chalmers."

"Too bad. But that way you can have sprouts in bed if the fancy takes you. Ha!"

The lift door opened. With her stick pointed ahead, she stepped out deliberately, as if across a ravine. She turned, and patted her pocket again.

"We're thick as thieves, egg and cress, bubble and squeak." She raised a finger and pointed it between his eyes. "And we're going to keep in touch."

It was four forty-eight when Kyle joined the shoppers on the high street with no umbrella and no plan. The rain and the darkness half-smothered the festive lights, and along the kerbs the water gushed ready to splash. He'd had his mother all sorted, but now he was starting again on a budget. He wasn't sure she'd understand why he'd given her present to a crazy old girl and he didn't want to chuck any more money down the pan.

Another phone would clear him out. She'd be disappointed whatever he chose – short of some celebrity perfume. That was an idea. Kyle found the right section in the department store.

"Can I help you?"

The girl was almost Goth. Everything she wore was black: tight trousers, shiny shirt, bangle, ankle boots, tassel-type earrings and eyeliner. It made her lips redder and her eyes bluer.

"How much for a small bottle?"

"50ml?"

Wasn't that ten medicine spoonfuls? That'd last his mother a fortnight at the most.

"Forty-three ninety-nine. 100ml is better value," the girl told him. "Want to sniff?"

She sprayed her own wrist and held it out, narrow and very white.

"Nice," he said. He saw from her label that her name was Charmaine. She'd have been more impressed if he looked a proper chauffeur, with an ironed collar, shiny shoes and a designer smell of his own.

His phone rang in his back pocket. *Her*, already.

"Sorry," he told Charmaine, not expecting the little smile in reply. It changed her face.

"Hallooooo! Is that Kyle Green?" Her voice was so loud they probably heard her in Shoes. "I made it work! What you'd call a dummy run. Won't keep you."

"How's Room 23?"

"Surviving like me. TTFN and thanks again, Kyle Green. It's a lot of fun. Bye-eee!"

He grinned as he switched off. Now a pair of proper customers had got hold of Charmaine so he might as well leave it. He'd found it easier to chat to Gerry Chalmers than this girl with a pretty smile and that was sad but true. But then only one of them was barking. Looking back through the stands and shoppers was harder than spotting Wally. But when he glimpsed Charmaine he thought for a second that she was searching too. For him?

A girlfriend would be nice. His record was three months with Karen and it was six months now since she'd dumped him. One less present to buy. He wondered whether Gerry regretted going solo in the world. Like his mother must regret him, whatever she said.

Stepping out into darkness he felt the phone vibrate sneakily in his pocket.

Is this a text? Jolly clever. Testing testing. Over and out. She'd even added a smiley.

It is, and you are. You've passed, ten out of ten. She'd love that. *Have fun.*

Kyle wasn't sure how much fun she could have in a hotel like that on her own. She'd chosen it because it was *on mute.* To be her stage?

He hadn't pressed Send yet. He had an idea, another mad one.

Am buying a present for my mum. What's the best thing no one's ever bought you?

The market traders were starting to pack up, rescuing dresses before they got blown into a puddle. A guy called out, "Twenty quid, mate. What size is she?"

For a moment he pictured Charmaine before he remembered his mother. "Yoyo dieter, mate!" he called.

Yoyo mother too, he thought, but doing well. The previous Christmas she'd still been on anti-depressants. He hadn't told Gerry that bit, but if anyone had a right to depression at Christmas wasn't it her, in Room 23?

As Kyle crossed the road another text came through. *World's a nicer place in a beautiful balloon. Adventures are good. G.A.C.*

Genius. She'll love it.

Kyle ducked into a covered alleyway and tapped in *Hot Air Balloon Flights,* hoping they were 95% off in winter. It could be her birthday present too. But who said mad was bad?

Gerry never slept well on the first night. Her stomach tended to be all over the place. She'd aim to tackle the greed in a gradual sort of way once she'd got a few more puddings down the hatch. By the last morning she'd astound them all by saying, *"A grapefruit, please – no, make it a half!"*

Day Two was for settling and brushing up on bearings, patrolling the hotel on what she called a reccy, looking out for little changes here and there. She liked to show Martin Hedges she was as sharp as ever: *"You've painted the radiators,"* or *"Lovely spot of upholstery on the piano stool, Martin!"*

At the end of her tour with the stick to keep her steady, she sat down for coffee and told the size 14 girl in the size 10 clothes that whatever they'd paid for the brand new angel on top of the tree, they'd been robbed.

"Glitter and beauty, you know," she added. "Two different things."

The girl looked disgruntled. A sourpuss. "Nothing personal," she said, squinting at the girl's badge, "Torah. Jewish name, is it?"

"Toy-yah," said the girl, almost shouting. It made Gerry wince. She had to recover before she could resume her patrol, hail the staff, wish the other guests well and read her *Times* before lunch. The weather was dire but she had something to amuse her now, between articles. Textese, they called it, and it was rather jolly.

The other guests are a motley crew. Man the lifeboats! Heaven help us all.

Hope you packed your rubber ring, Kyle Green replied.

There was Fred Astaire to tap her feet to in the afternoon, and then four naughty courses to make her tummy rumble and her heart burn before bed. Back in her room she congratulated the roses. They were holding on gamely, survivors after all.

Not many laughs at dinner, she told Kyle.

You'd better put on a show, he answered. *Tap shoes? You've got the cane.*

Might have to use that, she wrote, *on one of the waitresses.*

Once she'd made it into bed for a zappity game or two, she told her legs they were as stiff and heavy as cabers to be tossed for Hogmanay. If only they would follow orders she could probably remember the steps of a few reels. She danced with Fraser at a Ceilidh but she wasn't one for moon and stars or hanky panky either and words were cheap in the end.

"Could have loved him forever but it's too late now."

Silly to get shot of the letters after all this time. But the milk was spilt now and she wasn't one for crying. She glanced at the phone and knocked a few little skittles flying. Kyle Green had told her to turn it off at night so he couldn't call her by mistake from a club at two a.m.

"Do as you're told, Gerry. That's a first."

But thinking gave her more trouble than usual, on top of mulled wine pears with berry fruits. At two a.m. she was still awake to think of him, look at the phone and whisper, "Behave yourself like a good bus stop!" Funny business, really, that she had a spanking little gadget by her bedside at last and the only person she'd called on it was a long-haired boy with no classical education and more cheek than a whole dorm at bedtime.

Struthers Minor had called out *"Mummy!"* when his fever was highest and she was just Matron. Of course Struthers was born too soon and nowadays they'd open up his brain and solder the ends together but getting people to think was a different matter. Kyle said the games on the phone were good for that. Maybe she was over-stimulated. Better knock herself into dreamland with the stick.

When she woke next morning, she felt discombobulated. She'd have to get her skates on because Christmas Eve had started without her, but she'd check the phone first. Turning it on, she realized she could call that nephew of hers and let him know she was alive and learning. Mr Ragged Robin Chalmers Esquire would get the shock of his life and that would teach him.

Greetings, Christmas Robin. It is I, your auntie Geraldine, and this is a text message. Same time same place and C U 2moro.

Grinning, she sent it on its way. Dull chap at the best of times so he might not see the joke. But then you couldn't choose family and he wasn't what she'd call her greatest fan. After a shower she was about to put her phone in her handbag when it exploded into a demented rhythm that made her drop her stick on her bare foot.

"What the Dickens are you doing to me, Kyle Green?" she cried. "I can't hop the way I used to. Life's not a Ceilidh." She pressed the button. It wasn't him. "Yes? Miss Geraldine Chalmers speaking."

"Ah, Gerry."

It was Robin, sounding less than chipper even before he coughed.

"You're not coming."

How many times? 2013, 2010, 07, and worst of all 1999, when Hedges had brought her a message during her third apperitif, the table all set for two. Colds, bugs, flu, food poisoning. He was sicklier than Struthers Minor and it was time someone opened him up for some soldering.

What did she always say? *"Ah well, can't be helped. Get well soon."* Looking at the small, flat screen, she could picture him sitting at home with a mince pie and a sherry and a silly hat on his head, his cheeks round and red.

"I'm afraid I can't risk passing on these germs, Gerry."

"Don't spare me! It'll take more than a few weedy germs to flatten me.

Spare yourself the effort if you don't want to come. It's only Christmas. Doesn't bother me one ounce or iota. You stay in the warm with wifey and I'll eat your dinner, two. In bed."

Gerry pressed the key with a firm thumb before he could cough again. It was a weasel of a man who couldn't stand up to a harridan like that. Pity you couldn't take nephews back to the store and swap them for bubble bath.

"He had that coming," she muttered as she left her room. "Hold the lift and breakfast too."

Gerry rather hoped to avoid Martin Hedges because she didn't need his pity thank you, but she supposed she'd have to tell the kitchens she'd be eating alone. So at lunch time she informed Sanjay sotto voce, and added, "No need to tell the boss," raising one finger and winking by accident.

"Mr Hedges is off for Christmas Day," said Sanjay.

"No, hardly ever," said Gerry. She whispered, "Mrs H high-tailed and left him on the perch."

She was tempted to keep young Kyle Green in the picture about that wretched nephew of hers, but there was dignity to consider. Not that he had a drop of it.

Don't forget to put your stocking out l8er. Happy Christmas Kyle Green from G.A.C. and C U soon.

It was a way of saying she wouldn't bother him on Christmas Day or Boxing Day. She'd bother the little Martians on her phone instead and they'd better watch out.

Martin Hedges woke to his day off. He rather wished he'd fought when the staff ganged up on him with talk of his "turn" to have Christmas Day with the family. Maybe he shouldn't have bandied that word around as if he had one worth mentioning. He hardly dared check the TV schedules in case there was no *Morecambe and Wise* to make him laugh later in the same old places. He opened the fridge on a pack of spicy sausages, plenty of sprouts, three carrots and a couple of large potatoes. Preparing and consuming Christmas Dinner would occupy him for approximately twenty minutes.

He might as well be old and batty, he thought, like G.A.C. – the only person he knew who wanted to sound like a bank. Her clothes only pretended to have been discarded by a bag lady; the labels that often stuck out spelt a different message. Then again, she had no car and The Excelsior was apparently her only holiday each year. Could she be one of those wealthy old spinsters who didn't see the point in knocking around in a mansion when a flat was easier to clean? But who would inherit the money she didn't spend?

The only answer Martin could think of, as he percolated some coffee, was the appalling nephew who let her down so regularly. And was no fun when he did appear, with one eye on his watch and more interest in the food and booze she paid for than the company.

And who will benefit, Martin Hedges, when you shuffle off this mortal coil?

In his head she asked the question in her enormous voice, still thick and dark with whisky and smoke even though these days she only indulged in puddings and a single Emva Cream. It would be banter but it would have a point all the same. They were in the same boat, and for all her craziness, she knew it.

Martin gave up a radio search for a cathedral choir and cut off Slade. He supposed his sister would call at some point, drunk as a skunk, with a riotous soundtrack providing her excuse to ring off. His brother would text with such civil goodwill that anyone else might be taken in and think he gave a damn. And his own reply would be equally convincing and just as insincere.

He should have asked G.A.C. to give him her new mobile number. But she'd rather hear from the larky lad she'd known for all of five minutes than a man she could mistake for the wallpaper.

By the time Kyle surfaced, the turkey was already in the oven and his mum had her apron on.

"Got any sprouts that need seeing to?" he asked her. He hoped she'd like her surprise present even more than a new phone. And that his present from her would be money to patch up the hole it had made in his finances.

"Happy Christmas babe," she said, and put her arms out for a hug. "You can peel some parsnips, cut them skinny."

"O.K." Looking at the clock, he thought it would be a good time to send a text.

"New girlfriend?" asked his mother, crossing her fingers in the air.

"Not exactly," he replied, and grinned.

Festive greetings, he told her. *Keep those windy sprouts under control.*

He'd heard her in the car, bubbling below the sat nav. He didn't fancy getting old.

Martin hadn't planned to spend Christmas morning driving in search of a petrol station that sold potatoes, but then he hadn't expected his sister's call to last long enough for the ones he was parboiling to dissolve.

"I'm packing my bags, Mart," she'd announced. "He's cheating on me. And I've got no winter coat."

At this point there had been shouting in Spanish. Martin wouldn't know whether José was defending himself or dishing the blame, but she shouted back in tearful English that he had no heart or conscience. Martin could hardly ring off and let them negotiate a language.

Then she took the phone outside and listed the neighbours she couldn't expect to put her up on Christmas Day, interspersing the names with swear words to fit José, so he had to wait his moment. Three times he'd tried to recommend communication and warn against acting in haste before she'd agreed to try. Now, setting off in the car, he imagined how he'd cope if his sister ended up on his doorstep with a hat box, foot spa, fake tan booth and flat screen TV.

The first three garages were potato-free zones that only earned him the kind of looks from the cashiers that young staff gave Geraldine Chalmers behind her back. Considering where to try next, Martin found himself round the corner from The Excelsior.

Why not? He'd get to see Toyah's singing gran in the flesh.

Gerry had never imagined in all her born days that there could be so much technicolour twaddle on TV. It still wasn't twelve thirty and she'd made coffee last as long as possible, with three mince pies, but really Christmas wasn't what it used to be. Thank the blue blazes for her phone. Now, nothing too wild and whoopy. Scrabble would keep the wires straight.

But somebody out there got all the best letters and she couldn't zap them for it. It was Christmas Day and she couldn't be expected to hang around all day in this room like a scarecrow with no birds and no corn. Time to bundle herself off to the lift and make do with sherry. Emerging, she borrowed some tinsel waving around an old landscape and, standing her stick against the wall, attempted to tie a spiky red halo on her head. But as soon as she started to walk it dropped and sat on her shoulders like the fox fur her grandmother wore for church on Christmas Day.

Waylaid by Sanjay, she agreed to an aperitif at the bar.

"Turn the music down, Deejay," she said. "Santa never had a baby. Don't these people ever read the Bible?"

"It's live music, madam," he pointed out, but she could hear perfectly well that it wasn't Jonny.

She glanced across at the grand piano but the music must be out of a box because no one sat in a dinner jacket behind it. Cavorting in front of it, the singer seemed to think she was some kind of snake wiggling out of a basket. No spring chicken anyway. She had a messy perm and a clingy red dress that mapped her bumps and rolls.

"Some people should look in the mirror," she said, squinting through the glasses low-slung towards her nose, "before they leave the house."

Ah, volume slipped? Someone coughed in a schoolgirl kind of way but people had no dignity. The chanteuse who wanted all sorts of silly nonsense from Santa must have white hair too, once you washed out the yellow. Spades were better off being spades. No use trying to get them to trim your toenails.

Her magic phone could remind her to book her chiropodist and Kyle was going to give her a lesson on the way home, so she'd have to give the old brain a bit of a clear-out. But why get rid of old Jonny? Martin should have told her; it was disorientating.

She took a while to settle on the edge of a leather armchair.

"Ah, bingo," she breathed. The singer kept pretending to flirt with Santa. She called that common but the guests were lapping it up.

When Martin spotted Gerry, she seemed to be putting on a floor show. Leaning her upper body as much as she could towards the nearest guest, she told him (and the rest of the lounge), "Jonny always tinkles the old ivories but he must be ill, or dead."

Martin wasn't going to mention Jonny's sudden rehab. Toyah's gran sounded all right to him; he liked a voice that had lived. Hanging back, he saw Sanjay take Miss Chalmers a drink. He also handed her a deluxe cracker, which she thrust straight back at him.

Her "KAPOW!" as she pulled it was louder than the snap, piano and vocals put together. Hecklers at a comedy club couldn't be more disruptive. Martin wasn't on duty now and his face took the liberty of rearranging itself. As the song ended he clapped enthusiastically.

"Ah, it's the cavalry to the rescue!" cried Gerry, hailing him with her stick. "The tone's been lowered around here, Martin. What happened to Jonny?"

He knew Gerry Chalmers had all the tact and diplomacy of a ten ton truck on the loose but who did she think she was? Listening to the almost triumphant bounce in her voice, anyone would think she was enjoying the license she gave herself to be cruel. He hoped Toyah's gran had thick skin as well as a powerful pair of lungs.

Martin wished he'd just slipped straight into the kitchen and sneaked away with a few nicely golden potatoes in foil. But now G.A.C. was patting the armchair next to hers, which was a noisy business. Toyah's gran was giving her the evil eye and she wasn't the only one. Good job Toyah wasn't there to find a few words to fit.

Sitting, he told Miss Chalmers he'd just dropped by to check things were ship-shape and was glad because he was enjoying the new singer very much.

"I've been bad, Martin," she said, and her bottom lip drooped. "No holds barred. Tell the lady I didn't mean it. Devil gets inside me and I'm in my green pinafore again, up to no good after lights out."

He could see that her eyes were moist and her cheeks burning. She really was sorry.

"I'll have a quiet word," he said. He'd have to think what the right ones would be but he did have the singer's number.

"Your nephew will be here any minute," he said, hoping to cheer Miss Chalmers now because she looked so deflated, even though he couldn't imagine that cold fish brightening anyone's day.

"Cried off," she said, and looked deep into her glass without drinking.

Her fingers looked thick enough to grab an Alsatian by the throat but her hand shook a little. He hadn't noticed that before.

"What a shame," said Martin. "Dinner should be a treat."

Was it his imagination or wasn't he quite up to the managerial persona without the suit and tie? He felt as uncomfortable as she looked, and also rather hungry.

"Will you join me, Martin Hedges? My bill, of course."

Martin hoped he didn't look as thrown as he felt.

"That's very kind," he said, "but I'm expecting my sister. She's split up with her Spanish boyfriend." He looked at his watch. "I'd best be off. She'll be landing at Heathrow in ... well, rather too soon. I'm meant to be picking her up."

He might be imagining it but he thought the Chalmers eyes hardened even though they were still glinting with remorse. He had an arrival time in his head, ready. Martin stood and wished her a very happy Christmas.

Three minutes later he was back in the driver's seat. He looked at his face in the mirror. Why? Such a shabby lie. What made sitting down at an immaculately laid table with a lonely old woman a more appalling option than a third class plateful in his own kitchen, with mince pies from a box, no crackers and no tree?

Exposure. He'd run from it, which could be stupid as well as selfish.

Dismissing the guilt, he made a definite decision to call Toyah's gran after her set ended. She must be on her own too …

Soon after *Top of the Pops* (his mum's idea, not his) Kyle's sister Anne-Marie finally arrived with baby Darren. When they sat down to a turkey dinner Kyle found a text on his phone that must have come through during something loud that had his mum jumping.

The good old Excelsior has risen to new culinary heights. No wuthering to be seen. Lucky old G.A.C. Don't get too tiddlywinked and if you see Heathcliff send him this-a-way.

Was she tiddlywinked herself? He pictured her with her arms linked in a line of people with paper hats and streamers, doing the cancan around a piano. Back in the day, maybe she was a party animal. But even though her thick, blotchy legs and twisted feet would stop her dancing, the hotel staff would get the board games out after lunch. It must be the highlight of Gerry's year.

Kyle began to answer while his mum drained the sprouts.

"Hey, get off your arse, you, and stir the gravy."

"Just a sec," he said. He was aware of Anne-Marie rolling her eyes and muttering, "Useless," before she put Darren in his little chair and stirred the pan while he finished his message.

I'm scrabbled myself. Got to go as the sprouts are on the loose but will keep an eye out for maniacs reciting love poems outside the offie.

The quality of his texts was soaring, he told himself. In fact he was so proud of their literary merit that as they ate, he thought he'd tell the whole story. His mum crossed her arms and narrowed her eyes at the part about giving away the phone she'd been counting on, but when she interrupted he reminded her about the hot air balloon and she went floaty all over again.

"That was her idea," he told her, and performed the texts in sequence. Gerry's messages brought out his best acting since he played First Shepherd. His mother smiled all the way through; he ignored his sister's comments, like, "Is she cracked?" and, "Who IS this?"

"Here," said his mother, reaching for his phone, "I'd better check your spelling. Posh, is she?"

Kyle said she was earthy too. "And wild," he added.

Darren shouted on cue, and kicked hard for an extra-big bounce so Kyle cheered him.

"Very kind, sweetheart," his mum said. "It's good to know you'll look after me when I'm eighty."

Kyle topped up his wine glass, looked at his mum and tried to age her like a computer program could, but at forty-one she was still soft and smooth. Funny how some things were unimaginable until they smacked you in the face.

Did G.A.C. wake up each morning glad she didn't die in the night, wondering whether she'd make it through to the next bedtime?

On Boxing Day Martin found Geraldine Chalmers subdued and confessing a hangover but it couldn't be as heavy as his. Still, without Dutch courage he might not have called his new lady friend to compliment her on her set. No fluttering, he told himself, not at his age.

He'd never seen G.A.C. legless, which was just as well since it would take three youngsters to keep her upright. She showed him a game on her phone that he couldn't follow, and claimed to be addicted already. She was playing between courses at every meal, and in the lounge at coffee time he found her crying out in frustration, defeat or triumph like a nine-year-old boy. Every so often she'd cry out, "Take that, mi' hearties!" or "Geronimo!"

The next day she was collected at three as always – or rather, closer to quarter past. Her anxiety had been mounting while she patrolled the foyer with her stick, leaning on furniture. Kyle Green looked genuinely pleased to see her, but not as relieved as his passenger. She grinned broadly as she waved her stick towards him. One of the guests ducked like a bystander at an explosion.

"Oh thank the Lord, Kyle Green. Can't have all my chauffeurs dropping dead."

"Told you I'd be here. You got everything, then?"

"Not as many wits as I arrived with but if they find them lying around they'll post them on with my bed socks. Hiding from me, they are. Smell will guide their noses. Get the bloodhounds in, Martin."

She shook his hands as always, thanking him. Her grip was looser these days, and damp.

"Anchors away then. See you next year, same time same channel."

No point in telling her he wouldn't be here next time. Or thinking about how hard that might hit her. He stood and watched the driver help her into the car.

"Happy New Year, Miss Chalmers," he told her, before the door closed.

"And the same to you with bells on, Martin Hedges. Call me Gerry. Merry Gerry, charming very!"

Kyle Green gave him a smile as he closed her door, but it wasn't the kind people had given him before, private and knowing, questioning her mental health. The last exchange Martin overheard was her asking the boy if he'd started wooing Charmaine yet and him protesting, "Give me a chance! One girl at a time."

Remembering the roses, Martin went to her room and cleared the red petals that had fallen on the carpet. Feeling their texture between his fingers he pictured the garden his wife used to care for and the time he'd have to nurture it back to life.

On the third of January Mel called for Gerry Chalmers as she did every Thursday, and thanked her, as they set off on their usual "jolly jaunt", for the bag of Christmas presents that had touched her to the point of a tear. She knew emotion wasn't the kind of thing you confessed to Gerry, but she asked about her stay.

The smartphone Gerry pulled from her pocket astonished her.

"Best present I ever had. They have magic powers, these things. So watch it, Mel. Don't want you hopping home to the lily pond!"

Mel began a question but Gerry wasn't in the mood for dialogue. She was holding forth.

"Present from my grandson. Intents and purposes rather than blood and law and all that jazz. I bet there's an app to floss your teeth and get the hairs out of the plughole. There!"

She gave it a quick stroke before she zipped it up in her bag.

"Lucky you," said Mel. She'd never heard of a grandson but then after four years of walking down the high street to tick off what Gerry called "missions to accomplish" Mel wouldn't get far with a family tree.

"I've got it set on loud. He's meant to be letting me know what happens with Charmaine at the perfume counter. I told him you have to eat while the pudding's hot. That was my mistake at the Ceilidh, you see. You only keep the letters so long."

Before Mel could do a little prompting on the most interesting question from Gerry's past, she found herself being pulled into the road as her companion began threatening the advancing traffic with her stick. The car slowed to a stop to let them across and Gerry used the stick again as a kind of salute.

"People will behave with a smidgeon of encouragement," she told Mel. "Such a good lad, Kyle Green, for a bus stop. Short back and sides would do the world a favour, mind you. Needs direction. Teenage mothers don't appreciate that but I have a feeling she does her best, you know. I'm beginning to wonder, Mel, whether most people do. Got to be less of a grump and more what they call upbeat. There are games on it, too. You wouldn't believe it."

Mel wasn't sure she did. "Gosh!" she said. "So you had a good Christmas."

"And he called on New Year's Eve – not at midnight, thank the Lord,

49

but ten past ten it was – just to wish me HNY. BTW!" She chuckled. "Ha! It's a whole new world."

Mel had thought of Gerry more than once, in that hotel, feeling sorry that she had no one when her own house was full to the rafters. Gerry's was the best news she'd heard for a while, whatever it was.

"Solicitors first," announced Gerry. "Appointment to be made. Amendments, just desserts."

Mel opened the door for Gerry. The office still managed to look rather Dickensian.

"You wait outside. Wheels to set in motion. I hope the perfume girl doesn't snub him but he can bounce back. I'm the master at that. Two wiggles of a pig's tail."

Mel smiled as the door closed and left her on the high street, glad of the unnatural January warmth. Mentally she tried to frame some questions that wouldn't be too nosy – because Gerry hated that almost as much as help down steps from strangers and people chewing gum in the street. Then, before she could use her own more basic phone, Gerry reappeared.

"All right?" she asked. Gerry had been known to complain rather vigorously about the law, her dad's estate, courts and costs and "gobble-dygook".

Gerry gave her a nod that belonged in a pantomime, but all she said, after she'd looked at her shopping list and begun to devise what she called a "route and schedule" was, "Come on then, life's too short. You have to get rid of the clutter." She winked. "And dance."

You can find out more about the authors* who have read and reviewed a story in this collection at the end of the book.

If: A moment of madness, or an act of self-salvation? By doing the one thing that most of us fear, a woman finds redemption in this parable for modern times.

Bea Davenport, author* and journalist, Berwick upon Tweed, UK

If is a humorous and all too human account of one woman's attempt to be herself in a world where nobody pays attention to anyone any more. A very realistic and wonderfully written portrayal of human nature, and the some-times surprising goodness of the human heart.

Joanne Bowers, library and information adviser, Ipswich, Suffolk, UK

Surreal and comical, If is a story of self-revelation told with delightful imagery and word play. A walk to the shops becomes an enthralling and unpredictable adventure.

Brian Bold, author*, Watford Writers, UK

It's amazing how much you can pack into 4 pages! If is a small portrait of lives intertwined, and possibilities associated with parallel universes. A charming and slightly surreal miniature.

Sally Goodman, environmental consultant, North Yorkshire, UK

A poignant tale every woman over a certain age will relate to.

Dorothy Schwarz, Colchester, author* and journalist, Essex, UK

If - what a liberating read that was! I loved the sense that I was getting into the character's own twinkling heels and just sauntering down the high street without a care in the world. A delicious story.

Melissa Mostyn, writer and arts practitioner, Bucks, UK

If

Tess hadn't planned it. Monday could have had a theme tune simple enough to sing around the house.

If, on Sunday night, she hadn't been afraid to call Peter and hear the inconvenience in the word "Mum". If George had turned that morning to wave or smile on his way out, or the hoover hadn't cut out the second she plugged it in.

If she'd been more of a woman and less of a lady.

It wasn't a decision, but a moment: capricious, flung together, stream-lined. It just began, in the bedroom, with a chenille dressing gown untied and hung behind a door, followed by a quick scrabble at the bottom of the wardrobe for perfect shoes. The barely worn pair, in fact, that George called cheap – on account of their kitten heels and silver straps jewelled with 'gold'. Like the necklace she fastened they were cheating of course, but in circumstances like these it was important to hold one's head high.

Even then, she might have stopped there, laughed or cried and pulled on some knickers ... if she hadn't behaved with such relentless decorum for the whole of her socially responsible life. Or if, through the last few decades, she'd played herself for more than a scene or two, instead of slipping into role without the smallest drama. If George ever took his eyes from one device or another and found her, where she was, in that place where she used to really be.

Maybe if next door's cat hadn't fought a ferocious great crow the moment she looked out of the window. If, gliding regally down the stairs, she'd tripped on those pretty heels and knocked her brains out.

If the hibiscus on the kitchen window sill had chosen this day, of all others, to live.

In the hallway, the mirror by the front door survived the shock with no fault-line crack. Opening the door, Tess skimmed its frame. Without support or control, with no investment, protection, treatment or gloss, she met the air without a go-between. She was fifty-six, naked and free.

Picking up the bunch of keys, she threw them on the floor and stepped outside. Behind her, a pair of swaying cheeks threatened to detach themselves at the base and leave milk jellies wobbling on her doormat. Her breasts let out a suckery slap. Tess was out now, in the breeze and the world, her eyes ahead and her mouth lifting in a smile that might have stretched like dough into a laugh that never stopped ...

But she recognized that bark. It was the dog opposite, the one with a tongue that would feed a family at Christmas. A tongue that always looked determined to wrap itself around something tasty and squeeze the life out if it, if it didn't drown in saliva first. Tess stood at the end of her drive, watching the door open across the street and a velvety muzzle break out, sniffing and dripping – but just for a moment, before the owner lifted his finger and closed the door. No walkies just yet. Perhaps the "Colonel" had just solved the last clue in the *Telegraph* crossword: *Possessed by the Devil* in 7 letters? That would be *satanic*! At best!

Tess opened her gate and left it open for Jehovah's Witnesses or passing bears. There were a few people walking ahead of her but she took care not to check behind. Noticing a child skip, she attempted to follow suit and tripped off one heel into the corner wall. One breast had to be cleared of moss and brick dust before she could saunter on.

The high street was busy as usual with silent people. Tess felt overwhelmed by her colour, her shape and texture, her sounds. How long would it be before someone called her name? Or would she yell it with bloodied defiance, like Kevin Costner in his feathers when the soldiers beat him – except that in Sioux she'd be *Dances with Dusters* or just at the moment, *Wobbles with Bling*?

Feeling her flesh moisten she realised that she could have kept a hankie securely tucked under one boob. A spiky branch she usually breezed past offered her a challenge: to limbo-dance beneath it just to prove she could. But she rose too soon and scratched her nose. Oh, the elegance!

As she approached the high street, a fly buzzed around her stomach. She shooed it with a hand, muttering, "I ask you! I'm not quite rotting meat!" But the irritating thing persisted. When she stopped on the pavement opposite the bakery it landed and settled – in spite of her hissing, "Jam doughnuts that-away!" Since it was in danger of incarceration in the labyrinth of creases known as her belly button, Tess brushed it away with some force.

So she might almost have stumbled over the woman, who was folded like a deckchair across the kerb. On the road, shopping made a Tate Modern installation. Tomatoes spread like a pizza topping, flour peaked in a feeble white sandcastle and an egg balanced in a second's indecision. Through a small crowd Tess saw a paisley headscarf of the sort grannies no longer wore, dragged across a bruised mouth. Thin ankles and lace-ups angled out between the Bran Flakes and the seeded wholemeal – halting the traffic while dance rhythms sliced the air from car windows.

Tess was through and crouching. The rest made way.

"I used to be a nurse," she said, establishing a pulse. She laid a hand gently on the woman's warm forehead. "She'll be O.K."

Pale blue eyes opened slowly. The woman's smile edged wide and girlish. Cool, swollen fingers pressed her palm. Lips shaped a soundless, "Bless you dear."

"Indeed," echoed a deep voice her gran would have called gentlemanly, but when she turned she saw what those *Loose Women* would call a 'silver fox'. Still crouching with miraculous balance, Tess coloured – probably all over.

Someone clapped, a young mother cried and a fat man passing by asked beerily whether it was his birthday. Two teenage boys shuffled off, laughing from the waist in low-slung jeans that made them walk like John Wayne. Gelled heads down, they were looking at a screen.

"Has anyone called an ambulance?" checked Tess. "I've left my phone at home."

Assured that the paramedics were on their way, Tess smiled at the old woman and attempted to stand, but one heel appeared to be caught in a drain. As she stumbled, the silver fox reached out a hand. To a siren soundtrack she stepped out of the shoe and felt his denim jacket around her shoulders, smelling vaguely of trees.

"Your name, dear?" asked the woman before Tess could take her first uneven step towards home. "I'm Edie."

"I'm Tess, Edie," she told her. "Time to run before midnight strikes."

Now the paramedics were pulling up. Her dinner dance necklace was quite wrong for a jacket that cried out for a peace sign, so she thanked its owner politely and told him she must be off – the goldfish would be wondering where she'd got to.

Kicking off the other shoe to begin a solo Conga, Tess supposed he could find her. So could anyone, really.

If …

You can find out more about the authors* who have read and reviewed a story in this collection at the end of the book.

Ravelled tells a tale that I suspect is familiar to many of us: our first unapproachable and innocent love. This bittersweet story will make your heart ache for the child you once were. Beautiful, poignant, and elegantly written.

Dawn Finch, author*, librarian and president of CILIP, Herts, UK

'Nobody's ordinary ... we come from the stars,' says Mr Jones. For all who have been inspired by a teacher, for everyone who remembers the pangs of first love or the confusion of finding their own self, **Ravelled** is a celebration of the human spirit over the knots of the mundane. Sue Hampton is a writer who is able to speak with the authentic voice of an adolescent and create many magic pieces of dialogue. This well-crafted story will resonate with all ages.

Ginny Moodie, retired social worker, Hertfordshire, UK

A beautifully bittersweet evocation of misdirected first love and the search for self; the characters leap from the page and stay with you for days.

Izzy Robertson, author*, West Dorset, UK

Ravelled is a coming of age story about young discoveries and in particular the joy of reading poetry alongside the pain of first and unrequited love. Set in the Seventies, it encapsulates the language and mood of this particular era as well as pinpointing those familiar feelings experienced by teen girls across all of time. A great story.

Jo Coldwell, bookseller and book club founder, Essex, UK

Ravelled *is the completely engaging story of a teenager's rite of passage through a transformational love of her English teacher and poetry. I particularly liked Marilyn's voice, the teacher's idea to ask the students about their names (such a brilliant scene) and the speed up in time towards the moving finish. Life is not poetry but poetry can offer salvation.*

Hazel Ward, retired FE English teacher, Hertfordshire, UK

Sue Hampton has done it again. With her sensitive and uncomplicated story-telling skills, she has transported me into the character's world and left me thinking of delicious lines such as, 'It's poetry even while we struggle for words to recreate it'. Bravo!

Miriam Calleja, pharmacist, artist and author*, Malta

An interesting story, sensitively told. Hampton handles the age-old problem of teacher-pupil transference with common sense, tenderness, and understanding. I recommend this story.

Beth Heywood, writer, Northamptonshire, UK

As I got into Ravelled, *I was thoroughly captivated by the creative and descriptive language. With its unpredictable conclusion, it was an intriguing story line, capturing ageless teenage fantasies.*

Kaye Andrews, retired nurse, Bloomington, IL, USA

Ravelled

She was the only Marilyn in seven hundred and fifty girls. In her class there were four Susans, three Annes and some Janes, Janets and Janices, but her name set her apart. It was modern, with an aura of sophistication – even though she wondered why her parents had called her Marilyn at all, if they wanted to treat her like a Jane and insist that school rules about make-up and uniform were there to be obeyed.

But when she came home at four o'clock each day, her mother would ignore the brown mascara she'd applied to her lashes in the Girls' Toilets before registration, as if she only saw what she expected or wanted to see: a good girl who happened to be blonde. Marilyn made sure the school skirt with its rolled-over waistband was always lowered to skim her knees as she stepped off the bus, but she didn't tell anyone at school just how old-fashioned her parents were – or even how old. In twin sets and pleated nylon skirts, her mother might as well have been a gran; even the younger teachers wore shifts that showed their thighs. Marilyn would never waste herself like that. She was going to flaunt what she'd got.

By the Lower Fifth, the status her name gave her had been raised by another accident: the size of her bra and the tightness of her white blouse across it, with a button or two undone. "Oops, popped again!" she'd tell the teachers on patrol, adding a helpless, "Sorry!" Over that year she grew taller than most of her peers. Her friend Lorraine said she could get served in a pub with lipstick and a casual cigarette. But, for all her big ideas, Lorraine was five foot three and freckled. So Marilyn had no one to go along with such Let's Pretend, or make it real. Not even a boy.

Everyone assumed she was well practised in French kissing, but that was because they didn't know the way her parents imprisoned her in the name of protection. Most of her classmates lived close to the school and some went to the same Youth Club. Marilyn was the only one from Wickford, far enough away for her to keep the restrictions of her life a secret while everyone assumed she was out snogging in a dark corner with a Sixth Former in an ankle-length Afghan coat. And she had the

58

vocabulary necessary to sustain the deception, including the word that made her parents shudder if they ever heard it in the street: the F-word that spelt instant detention. She enjoyed the sound of it, and the frisson of disapproval that followed it.

"Who likes fucking?" she printed in a note she passed around in Latin, to see who blushed and who dared to answer *"Me"*. She watched the progress of the folded note from one desk to another, noting who smiled, who was startled and who looked around hoping to identify the author. Marilyn just continued to stare at the clock above the teacher's head, eyes dulled – even when she saw, in a sideways glance, a quiet girl (one of the Lindas) write something behind a curved hand. But the girl in the next row was an Anne who went to lunchtime C.U. and had apparently met her so-called boyfriend at church. This Anne scrunched up the little scrap of paper in her fist before she dropped it on the floor and kicked it towards the wall with the side of her lace-up shoe. All Marilyn could do was target the back of her head and hope that the front of it was crimson. If holy Anne had to wreck her research she could at least have told the teacher. That would have made an entertaining diversion, embarrassing Miss Needham, who was unmarried at something like fifty and wouldn't know the answer.

As it was, Marilyn stifled a disappointed yawn, slipped from her desk her copy of *Saturday Night, Sunday Morning* and began to read when she could. The couple in bed on the cover were either post-coital or about to begin foreplay; the photograph was a furtive talking point. Marilyn's mother had been appalled when she found it in her school bag, and even more shocked when Marilyn said, "It's a set text," and smiled because that was so close to the s word they didn't say, not in her house. It was a funny story to tell the others, and her mother said she would write to the school to complain, but Marilyn didn't suppose she had. She'd shy from the words she'd need to shape in her own handwriting on best Basildon Bond.

Her teachers avoided words too: *"An intelligent girl who could achieve a great deal more should she see fit to apply herself"*, *"quick-witted but less than industrious"*, *"Marilyn's attitude to her studies leaves room for improvement"*. When she was aiming, within limits, to be rude. To show that she didn't care. That school was just petty and the teachers were so dried-up it was impossible to imagine them doing the deed – even though Caesar must have, in between fighting the Gallic Wars. Her parents always said, when the report book came home, "We were hoping for better this time," so she always pointed out the percentages: nothing below 68, Division One for everything and sixth or seventh in class, all without trying. The numbers carried some weight with her father, who was a tax man, but all her mother wanted was nice manners, good behaviour – "You never smile, darling, and you have such a pretty smile."

Marilyn said she couldn't help it if the teachers thought her mouth looked sulky. *Sexy* was what she meant. Too sexy for Miss DCHS (Derston County High School) because all they wanted was a girl with lots of white teeth and a private school voice who could open the Summer Fair without wearing anything too far out for Princess Anne. Sometimes Marilyn practised pouting in the bathroom mirror, trying to look like Julie Christie with full, Nivea-creamed lips and thick hair falling on her naked shoulders. Maybe when she was fifteen she'd be allowed on the train to Carnaby Street and the Kings Road. She'd need clothes to fit in but by then she'd have a Saturday job. She wouldn't mind working in the new Wimpy Bar, next to the record store with the listening booth. Then life would begin.

But her parents didn't want her working in the town. Her father said he'd pay her the going rate to clean his car, cut the grass and weed the borders. And she had to listen on Mondays to the stories Janice told, about her job on a beauty counter and the "dreamboat" manager who told her she was a natural.

So Marilyn spent her so-called wages on cigarettes that she lit as soon as she turned out of the street. Standing by the bus stop with her skirt up to her thighs and a sour stare, she smoked where she could be seen by neighbours and reported. To serve them right.

But there was no scene, in spite of the smell that clung to her hair. She more or less gave up, and bought albums instead, the kind her parents hated: *Hunky Dory*, *Sticky Fingers*, *LA Woman*. In her room she played them on her little deck and danced as if Jim Morrison was holding her, one hand on her bottom as she swayed.

By the autumn of 71, when a boring summer came to an end and her parents pointed out how serious the Upper Fifth would be, with 'O' Levels at the end of it, Marilyn told her diary that she was in prison and if she didn't find an escape route soon – like Lorraine, who was in Australia – she'd probably set the place on fire. At the bus stop on the first day back at school that September, she noticed, among the boys passing by on their way to St. Ignatius, one who'd transformed over the holiday from a boy to a dish. If he'd been Upper Sixth, she might have smiled at him when his friends called her "a Pan's Person" and he looked concerned about their manners. Marilyn just showed them a couple of Flick Colby swerves that sent them laughing on their way.

Arriving at school, she heard the rumour that the new Head of English was a man. Someone had seen him with an old briefcase and mac, hurrying from the station and almost late on his first day. "Oh, at least forty" was the estimate, greeted with groans.

"It says on the job ad," said Marilyn, and switched to her Headmistress voice, "Applicants any sexier than the Prime Minister will not be considered." A few people thought that meant Wilson but Marilyn knew better because her parents liked Heath and called him a gentleman.

Still, it was disappointing to have no English timetabled for the first day, but in the dining room people said Mr Jones was "really funny", "outasite!" and "so sweet". So as U5H class waited for him to arrive next morning, in the upstairs classroom overlooking the newly-mown field with the tennis courts beyond, Marilyn felt more interest than she showed.

Using his pregnant-looking briefcase to hold the door open, he struggled in with a pile of books balanced under his other arm. Everyone stood but he said, "Oh, no need for any of that," the pile broke up and tumbled; girls picked up the scattered paperbacks. Marilyn watched. The title on the black cover was *The New Poetry*. As the copies were passed around he introduced himself, spelling his Christian name in chalk (and very bad handwriting): Bysshe Jones.

"Weird, you're thinking?" Someone laughed. "My parents were Shelley fans," he explained, "who believed in standing out from the crowd. I hated them for it – and at university I claimed to be Mike."

His shoulders went back, his chin up. People giggled. "You grow into yourself in the end. Names represent us out there, whatever identity we construct for ourselves in here." A hand flicked the side of his head where the curls were glossy in spite of the only kind of haircut that would get him through an interview. "I need to know yours, and how you feel about that."

The girls looked at each other, smiling in surprise. He looked at the nearest Anne, the God Squad one, inviting her to begin. She hesitated. Marilyn noticed the imperfect edges of his brown shirt collar and the woolly texture of his modern art tie.

"Do we get an action replay, sir?" asked someone. People laughed. "I missed the question."

"Answer your own if you wish," he said, "but bear in mind that this is only a double lesson and the idea is to dive into some poetry before break time."

Anne began mumbling about her name because she didn't know what to say really, apart from how "ordinary" it was.

"Are you ordinary?" It was a flicker of a question. Anne coloured, and pressed the spine of her glasses back. Barriers up.

"Probably."

"I don't believe it! And you mustn't either. Nobody's ordinary." He picked up the poetry book. "This here proves the ecstasy of agony. How full emptiness can be. We come from the stars – nothing ordinary up there!"

His finger pointed upwards and a couple of girls even looked at the slightly grubby ceiling. Marilyn felt the warmth of a grin on her face. He was loco and she loved it.

Now he was naming famous Annes and asking Anne Clegg to pick one she connected with.

"Boleyn," she said, and blushed at the giggly gasps. Mr Jones reached out a hand that silenced it all. He was waiting. "It's sad," she said.

"Tragic heroine or manipulative go-getter? Or both? We can never really know, and yes, that's sad – and bottomless too. You've been reading Jean Plaidy." The hand stopped her answering. "That wasn't a charge. Confessions are best turned to poetry." He waved the book, one finger pointing at the centre of the cover.

Marilyn listened as Janet said she had no Janet to identify with at all, and Mr Jones said, "Ah. Rochester calls Jane Eyre 'Janet', in tenderness as I recall. Judge for yourself whether a victim can be a heroine. And whether like Darcy he's a legitimate heartthrob. Who's yours, Janet?"

She shrugged, and her neighbour showed him her wooden ruler, decorated with the names of lead singers he said he was afraid he hadn't heard of: "Dean Ford?" to a chorus of "Marmalade!"

"You don't need to know," Marilyn muttered. And he heard, looking straight at her, just for a moment. She knew her turn would come. And some of the others had so little to say – even though it was so much more than they'd ever revealed in a classroom before.

The cleverest but most silent of all the Susans said she wasn't Susan at all, but Sue. "Only teachers call me Susan, because they don't know me." Her voice fractured. "It's not me they're talking to."

There was a thick pause of astonishment after that, while Susan reddened to the roots of her frizzy hair and Mr Jones smiled, nodding. "I shall try to earn the right to call you Sue," he said, quietly, seriously, "because I'd like to know you."

His smile was boyish. Marilyn could imagine him at school, 'full of beans' like *Jennings* but knowing things without swotting. He thanked Susan for her honesty, adding that without that there would be no poetry. Then circling his forefinger and landing it on the register, he looked up and asked, "Marilyn?"

He wasn't handsome; his eyes had a froggy bulge and his teeth were a jumble, almost puffy. Marilyn didn't need to raise her hand because all the others had turned; she was in focus.

"Ah," he said. She wanted him to know her, better than Susan, and she had an idea that if she just gazed straight back at him, he could see inside her. But what could she say? That her name made her cheap, a tart like the character in *Crossroads*?

He began, "Norma Jean – a tragic heroine for our times? More innocent than Anne Boleyn and more vulnerable," and had to explain what he meant. When he called Arthur Miller "a great playwright", and said Monroe must have been clever too, Marilyn had never felt more stupid, because she knew so little about this actress he seemed to admire, and her parents certainly didn't like it hot (if at all).

"I'm sorry," said Mr Jones. "I jumped in. I shouldn't have."

She shrugged. If she chose silence now, would that make her fascinating? "I've never known whether to live up to my name or down to it," she said, and although her voice didn't crack like Susan's she felt suddenly sad. It was as if everything she'd counted on had vanished. She didn't want to work in the Wimpy Bar, or lose her virginity to a Sixth Former, get spotted by a modelling agent or hitch-hike around the States in a mini skirt, with strings of beads around her neck and enough cash to buy some grass and see how it changed her. She just wanted Mr Jones to like her, but not the same way as the boys in the street. She wanted his respect, his understanding, his time.

"What do you want your name to say?" he asked, his voice gentle, curious.

"Confidence," she said, afraid of losing it. "Independence. The opposite of tragic and vulnerable." She remembered her mother's sniffiness about 'bra-burners'. "Liberated."

He nodded. "Bravo. I'm relying on women like you to demand your space and be heard."

Women like her. If she could hold his hand and walk in the woods she'd be real at last. Mr Jones said he didn't want any of them living or dying like Sylvia Plath, whose work was in the collection, but that writing could give them a voice and that was power. Words, he told them, reshaped everything.

Then he said he couldn't resist poetry any longer. "A love poem by Adrian Henri," he said. "A pop song without a tune." He pulled a slim volume from the inside pocket of his olive green corduroy jacket, thumbed quickly and read: "Without you every morning would feel like …?" He slapped the book down on the nearest desk and held out a hand, cupped but with fingers wiggling.

"A winter Monday." Someone said, "A power cut," and another girl said, "A train with no wheels," which made everyone laugh, Mr Jones loudest of all. Marilyn wanted to offer a line he'd always remember, a line to make him forget the ones in the book. She thought furiously, impatient with her slowness. Then she raised her hand.

"Marilyn?"

"Without you every morning would feel like dancing on jelly."

Someone spluttered. She heard it echoed. But Bysshe Jones tilted his head to one side. "Wait …" he said, and she could see he was excited.

"You know, you can't balance," she said. "And you're a mess. You're really only dancing because the jelly wobbles you around. You feel ridiculous."

"Ah yes, and it makes us think of childhood parties but this is the opposite, a kind of torture."

Marilyn nodded. She was in love.

At the end of the two hour lesson, the girls were slow to leave the room, but Marilyn didn't want to hang around like a twelve-year-old at the stage door after an Osmonds concert. She just walked away, running her fingers through her hair, remembering that her line wasn't wrapped in brown paper on anyone's doorstep, like in the poem. It was in his head. He'd be going to the Staff Room now, to share it: *"Is she gifted, Marilyn Green? She reminds me of Lara at the start of Zhivago."*

The weather was still summery enough to sit on the grass, so she took out her copy of the anthology and saw there were only two women in it. But in the nearest conversation, the female in question was Mrs Jones – whether there was one, and what she might be like. Why she didn't iron his shirt better! Irritably, Marilyn moved away. Weren't they inspired?

That night she spent four hours on the homework he'd set them: to find a poem they loved, and write as honestly and thoughtfully as possible about what it meant to them. She chose Larkin's *Wedding Wind*, read it aloud in her room three times, four, and wrote: *I love the wildness and the passion, the words like "thrashing" and "bodying-forth", the intensity of "the wind of joy" that makes him "sad that any man or beast should lack the happiness" he had. I love the idea of "perpetual morning shares my bed". It makes me think of a couple lying, warm and sleepy, with the sun shining on them as they kiss. It makes me feel like the bride, waking to a new world because I'm in love. The cattle ending seemed strange at first but then I realised what he's writing about is an animal instinct as well as romance, and love and sex are as natural and necessary as water. It's romantic, because he hopes the love won't "dry up" even in death, but wind can dry lakes so maybe he's afraid it might. We all feel the same about love, and we thread our beads on it knowing one snap and they spill everywhere. But when we find it we kneel, which for humans means worship, if you believe in God: someone to thank for the love and the loved one. If I could ever write anything as intense and beautiful as this poem I'd be glad I lived. As it is, I still feel "stupid in candlelight" most of the time.*

Her parents were incredulous – not that she let them read it; they'd lock her up for the rest of her life – that she should work so hard, and that her eyes were so bright when she explained, "I love poetry. When you go deep into it, it's the best thing ever. It's everything."

Only one thing mattered more to her than the way he read poetry, talked about poetry, used his hands to accompany poetry, and the words that sang and shone, and darkened and remained mysterious. The following day it came, scrawled in ink under a vigorous A+.

I applaud you for this genuine, well-expressed and open response, which is in itself as passionate and lyrical, but as honest too, as the poem. Even after a few hours of marking it made me return to Larkin's words and appreciate them even more. Thank you.

All, she thought, was "ravelled under the sun by the wind's blowing". Rereading the poem in bed that night, she could almost sense his hand under the sheet. Would she be "let to sleep"?

After half a term of poetry they switched to Shakespeare. "More poetry!" Mr Jones told them. "Everything's poetry. Look out of the window at that field, and the sky above it. It's poetry even while we struggle for words to recreate it."

Marilyn luxuriated in *Macbeth*: not just the text but the context he took them through with all their senses, the excitement and the shock of a new kind of love that fuelled murder. It made her daydream about ways of killing Mrs Jones to possess something more precious than a crown. If he were in love with her, that would be the only power she would ever need.

All her other subjects came more easily now. It was as if a window had opened and the light shone all around. She was able to show her parents – casually of course – A after A in her exercise books. They were like children surprised with sweeties. Her father rewarded her with crisp new pound notes and her mother said, "You won't smoke it away, will you darling?" but she had no intention of spending it on anything but books. Apart from eyeliner, which she wore to school unchallenged, and a red lipstick which she was saving ...

He was forty-two! He told them so, when someone asked. It made no difference; how could it? Every night, by torchlight, she added to a letter she was writing him – full of love, and struggling for words to recreate it – always remembering the importance of honesty, and of searching for deeper truths about her core self, and what it was to be alive. It was more obsessive than she had dreamed. Yet in spite of the closeness of him when she sat in the front row for the first time in her school career – "can't see the board," she explained, "but you can stuff specs" – they hadn't touched. She knew, in her loneliest moments, that it would never happen, but she must long for it anyway.

Christmas came and went, and Marilyn couldn't be sure whether he'd found the neatly-wrapped present she left on his desk in his Form Room – or recognised her writing even though she hadn't signed it. On Christmas Eve she started work on a *Without You* poem that began with the dancing in jelly but had grown twenty lines by morning. When her dad gave her tickets for *Hamlet* in the West End she burst into tears – and reviewed it afterwards for the school magazine Mr Jones now edited.

"Really incisive," he told her in January, stopping in the corridor an hour or so after she'd delivered it. "You gave such a rich, detailed sense of it, I might as well have been there."

"Wish you were," she said, before she walked away.

A couple of bitter mornings later, the Catholic boy she used to like came over to her at the bus stop where she was shivering, and asked whether she wanted to go to the pictures with him. She said, "Sorry, I've got a boyfriend," and gave him a smile that was meant to be kind. Girls talked about 'blokes' but the word didn't fit him yet. He looked disappointed but how could it be fair to snog with him in the cinema when her heart was taken – or at least, given?

It was unsettling when Janice, who was pretty in a doll-like way, got pregnant and left school as soon as her bump began to show. There was no official version, just rumours that the father, who might or might not be the dreamboat, was twenty-three and wouldn't marry her – so her dad chased him down the street, yelling. Marilyn felt sorry and envious at the same time. Anne Clegg got engaged and was planning to marry at a registry office in a long purple dress, so there was speculation that she was expecting too. Even the chubbiest, frizziest Susan had slow-danced with someone at a youth club – although she didn't want to talk about it, said she hoped he wouldn't ring and refused to tell Marilyn why when she asked.

The friendships Marilyn kept in school were even looser now that she loved Bysshe Jones too much to tell, and literature with a devotion that made reading – and her essays for him – a priority. But she preferred the company of the others aiming for the highest grade, so she could talk about love, betrayal and death on the page, and make warm, private connections they couldn't guess.

In the mocks she came top in English Lit: 88%. Lower in Lang but the teachers for that were mainly women, and she was fairly sure the youngest of them didn't like her. Mr Jones was already busy starring in panel games like *Just A Minute* or *Call My Bluff* for the girls' lunchtime entertainment, in rehearsing the Sixth Formers for an all-female production of *King Lear* and in playing vigorous piano for assembly, but she asked him to run a Writers' Group and he said, "Yes, of course. Poets' Corner.

Thank you, Marilyn – great idea." Now she could compose love poems and read them in the intimate environment of what was a kind of store cupboard for English text books, where the grouping of four or five chairs meant she could reach him, skin to skin – theoretically, if not realistically. The ecstasy of the agony.

"He shone a searchlight into emptiness," she wrote, and read aloud, "and filled it. In his eyes she found humanity. In his voice she heard music. In her bed she sensed him, lover-angel. And turned away, alone with tears."

In spite of the nervous fervour of her poetic exposure on Tuesdays, when she sometimes found herself troubled by the intellectual control of Susan's poems-as-exercises, no one asked questions. He must know her now; how could he not? Sometimes the certainty seemed almost enough.

Then in April, just before the Easter holidays began, her father interrupted her homework with an unexpected question. She looked up at the evening stubble that made her think of Fred Flintstone and realised he'd been sent. He was on a mission.

"Marilyn," he said, "we need to talk. Your mother and I ..."

"I'm not pregnant or on the pill," she said. "I hardly ever smoke and I haven't been sloshed yet. And I'm in the middle of an essay I need to finish before I draw up a revision timetable."

He flushed. She could see he was angry but she hadn't time for this. Her mother appeared, shadowy behind him.

"Darling," she said. "You work too hard. We'd like to see you go out with your friends. If you still want to apply for a job at the Wimpy Bar ..."

"I can't now. I've got exams in two months."

"It's not healthy," tried her mother, low volume.

Love wasn't, she thought, not love like hers, but she didn't suppose they'd know about that.

"You're not happy," her mother continued.

Happy? Something she'd never been, not since the sandpit days of dress-up dolls and a teddy on the pillow. Only with him, and Shakespeare and Austen and Hughes and Plath. Happiest of all when she was most hopeless, in Poets' Corner, his breath almost touching her cheek.

"I'm happy in my studies," she assured them, suddenly Oxbridge and

68

worthy of respect. "I'll celebrate my birthday when it's all over."

As they left her, it crossed her mind that they were characters too, if she knew their story. Meeting her mother on the landing before bed, she gave her a hug and felt the fragility of bones against her own softness. She felt alive.

The next day a rather dome-bellied Anne Clegg sat next to her in English and asked, almost in a whisper, "Will you come to the wedding? Not a bridesmaid but you know, for support? My parents won't be there."

"Sure," she said. She nodded to the door as Mr Jones stepped through it. "Invite him?"

"I could," smiled Anne. Everyone else loved him too, in their different way.

She came home that afternoon to find her parents had bought her a second-hand bike: "For air and exercise." She thanked them, because this was freedom too. Mr Jones lived in the next town and had mentioned a book shop there. She could cycle to the wedding – he'd approve of that – but would he turn up? No other teacher would consider such a thing but that was the point; he was a human being – "with brains and desires, ideals and shame," he'd said – and he understood that they were too.

The wedding was a few days after Easter. Marilyn told herself something would happen: a twin would be ill or his wife would need him to do some job even though he'd called himself 'a hopeless handyman'. She liked the way the hot pants looked with the loose flowery blouse tucked in, and her hair at its scented, blow-dried best. Managing to slip out of the house and avoid questions of unsuitability – not just of her outfit but a pregnant bride just turned sixteen – she cycled off in sunshine, glad it wasn't hot enough to sweat.

Apart from Anne in purple and her skinny groom in white, there was only the official in a cheap suit and Anne's awkward-looking in-laws-to-be. So Marilyn wasn't the only one who smiled when Bysshe Jones edged in, just as proceedings were about to begin. He was on the shoulders of the groom's brother, who might have come straight from a building site.

With the number of guests in single figures, Mr Jones looked around before sitting in the row behind Marilyn, a seat or two to her right. Marilyn didn't turn her head once through the short business of the ceremony. It was enough to know that he was well placed to see the black bra straps through her top and the length of her legs in nude nylon, but she was sad to notice the absence, on Anne's face, of the light that powered her now. The light she'd like him to see, and understand. Once it was over, he was the first to applaud. Then he followed her outside after the family. As Anne and her husband held hands for Polaroid photographs he murmured, "I need to go, Marilyn."

She walked with him a few steps to a bench, where she sat, crossing her legs. Smiling up at him, she shaded her eyes from the sun. There were red and yellow tulips in a round bed behind him.

He looked from the wooden slats to her, back at the newly-weds kissing for the camera and down on her again. "Such a shame," he said. "Her parents, I mean. I had no idea. And what good can it do?"

When he sat down next to her, Marilyn felt almost stunned. "I know." This might be the moment, the only one or the one that turned every-thing, and either way she couldn't seem to begin. She couldn't even lay a hand on his arm, or thigh. All those novels she had read, all that poetry of passionate being, and she had learned nothing. She might as well be a child. She was too afraid of his wholeness, the depth and breadth of him, his brain, his commitment, the life he'd already lived while she'd been posing.

When she lifted her eyes from her lap and met his, she almost cried.

"Marilyn," he said, and sighed. Such tenderness in his voice! "I know you think you're in love with me and how can I fail to be flattered? I'm honoured. You're extraordinary. And I don't mean this!" He smiled: a tribute to the physical reality of her next to him? "But it's not me. It's poetry you've fallen for."

Marilyn shook her head. Her voice was so small: "It's you too."

"I'm not for you, I promise. Trust me. In another life … well, I'd be a lucky boy. But not this one. I'm sorry."

He stood and she knew she couldn't stop him. Tears brimmed hot, and trickled. He was walking away and he hadn't even kissed her cheek.

"Marilyn?" called Anne. "Thanks so much for being here. Come to Den's house for sandwiches … Are you all right?"

She nodded. "I can't."

"Go on," said the brother, lighting a cigarette and offering the packet.

"You'd be welcome."

It did cross her mind that this could be when she found out whether she did like fucking. But she was extraordinary; Bysshe Jones was honoured; he might have loved her in a different life, romancing her with Keats. Theirs would have been *Wedding Wind*, not a quickie after nibbles once cheap booze smoothed the way. How had it happened for Anne – in the back of their dad's van?

She rose and smiled, made a kind excuse and thanked them, wishing them well.

"Will you still sit the exams?" she called back from the steps onto the street.

"Yeah! Lit anyway. Got to make him proud, haven't I?"

"Yeah," said Marilyn, and waved.

Over the remainder of the holiday she began revising. Learning the poems by heart lifted her to a place where she could reach her own images; soon the letter in her bottom drawer was fifteen pages long. The new term began, and it was only when she arrived for the first double Lit that Mrs Farrell thumped in with a longer skirt than usual trailing over Scholl sandals, and said, "Mr Jones and I have done a timetable swap so I'll be taking you through to the exams." She sat, a little breathless. No one spoke.

As soon as Mrs Farrell stretched a wobbly arm to the blackboard, Janet passed a note with no words but a face spilling tears. Marilyn pushed out her bottom lip. Whether he wanted to spare her or he couldn't trust himself, it was her fault anyway. She thought of Zhivago clutching his heart on the train, with Lara further beyond reach with each oblivious step. But this was different; she'd given him nowhere to go but away.

Cycling home that afternoon, past the pond on the common, she wondered how deep it was. Without him every morning wouldn't feel like dancing on jelly. It would be like winter fog, a wasteland, with always the same question: to die, to sleep? *I love you love you love you*, she wrote that night. Now there was nothing more. She folded the pages into a brick-like thickness and tied a ribbon around it.

At the end of her final paper some of the girls took her out to drink cider on the common. When the mother of the cleverest Susan parked her car to deliver a cake with sixteen candles, they hid the plastic bottles behind a bush. Then once the cake was cut and they'd sung a more drunken Happy Birthday than was strictly necessary, Susan said, "First love hurts but you'll find someone else."

Marilyn swore, had to say, "Sorry, Sue," and told her that she must be right but it was hard to believe in anything but poetry anymore. She almost added that he hadn't touched her, in case they imagined it the way she had, but then Janet asked, "Anyone we know?" so she shook her head, and let the tears run.

Two hours later she cycled home in a haze and was sick on the corner of her street.

On the last day of term she hid the letter in her bag and at lunchtime asked an Upper Third who was on her way to the Staff Room to deliver it to Mr Jones.

"All right," she said. "He's my favourite teacher. I wish he wasn't leaving."

Marilyn didn't stay to be officially dismissed in her Form Room. Not to be, not to be. The lessons were over.

She got eight As, including both kinds of English, and a C. Only Sue improved on that. Her parents couldn't have been more moved if she'd just survived a car crash, and when she called on Anne and the baby, she noticed her friend's results slip stuck to the fridge with A for English ringed three times in red.

"It was Mr Jones," she told Marilyn, feeding the baby from a bottle. "He made me care." Marilyn said she knew what she meant.

"How are things?" she asked Anne, because there were six of them in the house now, not counting a malicious-looking cat that caressed her bare legs.

"Oh, you know …" Anne looked out of the window to the deckchair on concrete, where Den was bare-chested and smoking with his back to them. "It's not poetry." With a smile Marilyn thought was brave, she turned to her blue-eyed daughter and asked her, "Is it, poppet?"

When Marilyn's first poem was published in a feminist magazine a year after university, she sent a copy to the school Bysshe Jones had moved on to, but it was returned "unknown at this address". She hadn't told her boyfriend; he'd see the humour but the pain would pass him by. But almost ten years later, when she won the Hartland Prize – only a small one – and was rewarded by a collection in print, she called it Ravelled. She was married then, with twins of her own, teaching full-time against her mother's wishes and her husband's too, drinking a little too much red wine and remembering each night and most days what Anne had told her baby.

The dedication read: *To Mr Jones with gratitude for immersing me in "all-generous waters". Love always.*

She hoped he might think the work extraordinary.

You can find out more about the authors* who have read and reviewed a story in this collection at the end of the book.

The Goddess *is one of the most exquisitely beautiful and poignant stories I have ever read: poetic yet utterly enthralling in its plot. It drips with sensuality like a sweet tropical fruit. It was so vivid it invaded my dreams for nights afterwards, yet like every good short story, this makes you start questioning – who defines beauty and how can society make such devastating pronouncements about who is or isn't beautiful when, like the joy it awakens in us, beauty can have no objective rules? As this story shows beauty can be found in absence as much as in presence. A forest is beautiful because it is full of trees, but a wild rolling moor is equally beautiful because it is bare of them.*

Karen Maitland, author*, Devon, UK

The Goddess: *There is beauty and there is difference – and they can be the same. In this lyrically-written tale, we see how a young girl's strangeness brings her power, hostility, fear – and love.*

Bea Davenport, author * and journalist, Berwick-upon-Tweed, UK

Sue Hampton's *writing is sheer poetry. You can but fall under the spell of* The Goddess *who holds her bald head high.*

Patricia Gerbaud, Alopécie France

A magical story of perception and how we see ourselves and how others see us. A lovely read.

Stacey Geddie, ex-pat living in Singapore with alopecia

The Goddess *is a beautiful read; I would recommend it highly. It gave me a sense of peace.*

Chantelle Scarvaci, alopecia, healthcare assistant, Maidenhead, Bucks, UK

The Goddess *is a brilliant short story based on the courage and will power of a girl called Nei Bubura. An emotional story that will definitely make you think too.*

Chloe Jones, student, Anglesey, Wales

The Goddess

Nei Bubura woke before the sea. Drifting dreamily, it breathed no louder than her sister in sleep.

Nei Bubura woke before the sun, while the sky was still purple but for the bright pink tails streaking through.

Her little sister lay still beside her, but for Nei Bubura each night was hotter and shorter.

Did they think she lived on light? Did they think her heart beat a different rhythm? That her lips were plumped with their own nectar?

Her people thought she had no fear. They trusted her, and like the pandan tree, their faith must bear sweet fruit.

But the rain so rarely came, and when it did, it teased the people out to paddle below the clouds with their coconut shells. The harder they pushed through spray in the fleetest of canoes, the faster the rainclouds fled.

They looked to her, for Nei Bubura was blessed. She was their queen, their holy one.

The young men shaded their lowered heads from the light of her beauty.

Yet each night the dreams of time to come snatched at her heart until it drummed like the rain that did not fall.

The first to rise, Nei Bubura drank in the morning but her throat was dry. The limp black hair of her sister clung to her head like seaweed to rock. Again and again she cut it but always it grew again, to gather sand and salt. As Nei Bubura stepped lightly past, she smelt the leafy scent of the hair that soaked the heat. She tried to remember such thickness, trailing out behind her as she swam, then weighted and dripping on shore. It had been so long.

Nei Bubura lifted one cool hand to the top of her smooth, bare head. It was her father who said the island itself was the shape of it, in the eyes of the birds above. And no one asked him how, without flying, he knew.

Purity, he said. A pearl, unblemished.

Clear and fragrant as fresh water.

The girl who rose above hair must be lifted above them all, a goddess to lead them through life and beyond where the dreams led on.

***

Nei Bubura had been afraid, at first, of the air that found her skin where it had been wrapped like other heads. In the waves that broke flat a moment on sand, she looked for her old face. No longer edged in flickering black it seemed so small, like peeled fruit, soft inside.

Is it me, she thought? *Am I who I was?*

Was I always a goddess, in hiding, growing up as one of them?

They were questions she never asked the father who placed a crown of whitest flowers around her head, their perfume filling her head in the heat and melting the sea and shore.

What if I am just a girl after all?

Now, without her father, she gave her own answers. She had been born among them to understand their fears, their vanity, their greed and sadness. But it was the hair she had lost that set her apart. It was a sign and a promise.

The soles of her feet were tough; the sand was fine and white. Nei Bubura looked up to the sky that was her birthplace. Purple would bleed into blue and the sun would glare through breeze to scorch the rocks.

Nei Bubura lifted her head and raised the palms of her hands out above the waves towards the breaking dawn.

Closing her eyes, she tasted rain on her tongue. She heard it tap on her scalp. She imagined it running down her cool, dry cheeks.

The goddess willed it.

If not today, then tomorrow.

Her power could not fail.

***

The coral island was green beneath the blue, and Nei Bubura liked to sit in the shade of the windblown palms when the fiery sun blazed on her bare head. Propped by roots reaching out of the earth and joining together to hold them tall in wildest wind, the trees grew heavy with fruit. Papaya, breadfruit and mangoes turned from green to yellow, orange to red as they ripened in endless sunshine. The juice would soon be thick and sweet and Nei Bubura's tongue would be the first to taste it.

Each morning, out on the water no one could drink, Nei Bubura's brother and his friends caught the fattest, most glistening fish. Each evening, Nei Bubura was first to be served around the fire, and only when she opened her arms to invite her people to join her in the feast did they begin to eat. But no one went hungry.

Now beneath the soil, Nei Bubura's mother feared for the pumpkins struggling to swell and firm in earth that grew grittier and more powdery with each dry day.

Nei Bubura smiled her thanks to the girls waving palms to cool her skin. She could rest no longer. It was time to dance.

Through the sound of the sea and wind she breathed the lightest notes she knew as her body bent and curved, leaned and swayed under a wide and gentle roof of pandan leaves. The girls who attended her rested their palms on rocks and danced around her. From around the island others came. Men, women and children, they bowed their heads as they moved. The black hair of women lifted like wings and flew.

But the head of Nei Bubura was unadorned and free. Like a blood moon in the night, it rose clear and high above the rest. The movements of the goddess were slow and graceful, her steps soft on sand. She arched her arms, crossed them, scooped up air. She stretched her long body as if to find the clouds and pick them. Her steps were quicker now. She flickered. She whirled like a tornado. Inside her head she felt the heat gather and fill the quietness. The island tilted. Her feet faltered.

Enough.

Above their heads the men carried her, and laid her down in the shade. The youngest, Kakiaba, felt too moved to look on her queenly face. Her eyes closed, Nei Bubura sensed his presence. Thinly she heard their voices praise her.

How great was her sacrifice. How beautiful her spirit. How pure her heart.

And when the rain fell, they would dance again, as they caught it in their mouths and fingers. They would give thanks to the goddess who loved them, the queen who had thrown their spears in the ocean so none might be afraid.

Nei Bubura closed her eyes. A fire burst above them and the droplets on her mouth had the salt tang of sweat.

Let it rain.

***

Later that day the breeze grew fidgety. Nei Bubura felt her people's eyes on her as the air cooled and rainclouds darkened on the horizon. Silently the islanders set out coconut shells, row on row, like farmers planting seeds. Nei Bubura waded into the sea, arms high. Her people stood behind her, waves washing their ankles, waiting for the rain to meet them. But they could only watch from a cruel distance as a blurred sky ran soft and wet, but out of reach.

Nei Bubura felt their disappointment like a scourge on her flesh.

"It will come," she told them.

In the night she thought she heard it, greeting the rocks with kisses. But perhaps it was just a dream.

In the morning the coconut shells lay empty.

The boy who loved Nei Bubura saw the sadness in her eyes and felt the weight of her burden. Sometimes he thought she was only a girl, different from all others, finer and purer in her beauty. Kakiaba wished he could hold her hand and stroke the contours of her queenly head.

As she walked proudly ahead, her wide, dark eyes on the sky, Nei Bubura heard his footsteps among the rest.

Sometimes, even for a goddess, it was hard to believe.

***

Through the day the heat grew thicker and the air thinner. Nei Bubura's small sister grew weak and pale. Nei Bubura could only stroke her

78

forehead and wave a green palm over her warm, dark hair.

She heard the wind scratch and tug, no more cooling than smoke. It smacked the rocks and made sand fly.

Nei Bubura had no eyelashes and her fine eyes stung. The island had no rivers, lakes or streams. The pools that bubbled up from below after rain lay dusty now. But she walked to each holy, life-giving spot and planted there the bare feet of the goddess. Out she breathed her pure, sweet breath into the scouring wind. Though she had little strength she found enough to dance, and sing. Around her, the people echoed her song.

When the pools shone wet, it was her duty to guard them. Now she could only fill them with hope. And the gift was not enough.

On her tongue she imagined the taste of Kakiaba's kiss. But she dared not meet the eyes of the boy who loved her. Nei Bubura was afraid that in them she would see reflected her own doubt.

Instead she walked out to a rocky ledge where the sea lay deep and clear below, stilled her heart and dived. It was her smooth bare head that met the water first, daring the coral outcrops to strike red, scattering the fish and plunging like a dolphin, streamlined and strong, under the surface. Above her the light danced starry. Nei Bubura was cool now. Her silk scalp rose up and out of the sea, and air filled her lungs.

See the queen of the ocean, she heard them marvel.

How she glides. How the rocks bow before her and clear her path. How the creatures of the sea gaze in awe on her beauty.

But Nei Bubura could not escape the drought in saltwater. She could only soothe her skin and grant herself a moment's peace from duty. Up to the sky she looked but its blue only dazzled. Even the goddess blinked away from the sun.

There was no wishing back the girl she used to be.

***

Striding onto the silvered shore, Nei Bubura ran her hand over her forehead and down to her long, bare neck. There the queen's gold coral lay, the rarest of all, with its own inner light.

There was no one like her and she must not forget it.

Sometimes she dreamed of strange men coming, men with washed-out faces. They wore heavy clothes to hide skin like fresh guano, and they watched with hunter's eyes. Nei Bubura saw the island stripped to dry bone, and water grey with poison.

She did not tell her people what she saw. But she feared that in those dreams she glimpsed a time to come, a time so far ahead no boat could reach it.

Only the shoulders of the goddess were broad enough to bear such burdens. Nei Bubura smiled on her people as she walked tall among them.

***

As evening shaded the *hollow land* Kakiaba wondered whether the goddess he loved felt the restlessness of her people. A fly buzzed around the mango he sucked even though its flesh was not yet soft and pulpy. The taste was bitter but sometimes it was hard to wait.

Nei Bubura had no wish to see another day melted into darkness without rain. But her people must not hear her sigh. Again she walked onto the shore and let the waves that traced its edges wash her feet. The sun was tired now and the colour was draining from the sky.

But surely it was too soon for darkness to scud in. It must be rainclouds that seeped, far away, through the faded blue. Somewhere showers were falling, and striking the waves that tossed them away.

Behind Nei Bubura a boat was tied to a rock. She heard it rattle with coconut shells as the wind licked around and bumped them. The men hung back, waiting for a word from the goddess. But this time she would not watch them bob away and chase in vain. It was for her to race the rain, and there would be no failure, no defeat. The wind would not challenge her. This time it would not drive the clouds away.

Kakiaba was first to drag the boat onto the water. Nei Bubura nodded her thanks and stepped on board. Taking the paddle, she steered a way out towards the grey skies, her bare head sprinkled by the spray. Foam whitened the crests of the waves whipped by wind. Her arms worked like a man's, their rhythm strong. She was a queen and she would save her sister. She would save them all.

***

On and on Nei Bubura paddled as the sea darkened and deepened with every stroke. Its swell was powerful, but so were the long arms of the goddess. Seawater speckled her cheeks and trickled down her bare head but it was the touch of rain she longed to feel, and it was close now. She could sense its freshness on the wild wind. The rainclouds could not be far away. Though the horizon outpaced her, slipping always beyond her grasp, the grey clouds above her drew near. They flowed towards her like a vast river with no bed. And soon she would be drinking from it.

As the waves reared, Nei Bubura felt the boat lurch. A sudden growl broke from the sky. A sharp needle of light pierced the cloud. And the rain fell on Nei Bubura, washing her bare head, her shoulders, her breast. It chinked and splashed in the coconut shells. Breathless, she let it fill her gaping mouth. But the wind was against her now, twisting the sea and lifting it high around her. The shells clashed and fought as the sea tried to break in and seize them.

See her battle, she imagined her people say. *See her courage and her strength. See the goddess overcome the storm.*

***

In her dream the people bowed to a man in black with a ring of white around his neck. The pages of fat black books were turned by wind but the shower that sprayed them was red.

Waking, Nei Bubura felt no power in her limbs. She was not kneeling but lying, limp as a dead fish, as if her guts had been stripped out and left her empty.

Opening her eyes, she saw feet encircling her. Sand clung to her body, cracking as she moved. Looking up, one hand shielding her face against the sun, she saw strange faces. The shouts she heard around her head were jagged, harsh. If they held words, she did not know their meaning. But she understood the message of the big male hand with fingers spread towards her. *Stop.* Or *No.*

These were not her people and the shores she glimpsed through squinting eyes were wider, rockier and more ragged. She had been carried like a fruit across the sea to an island she did not know. She heard the palms stir in the breeze but the trees were taller.

On the air she smelt the rain that had fallen here. Not so far away the pools would glint, warm and rich. But she did not know where, because this was not her home.

Staring down on her, the faces were not friendly. They did not know who she was and they were not respectful. Nei Bubura felt their eyes on her head, with its thin coat of sand. Suddenly it felt naked and small. She reached to brush the wet specks from her skin.

A finger jabbed towards her. The voices clashed. Someone laughed. Their heads were straggly with hair, every one of them, but they were not in awe of her beauty.

Nei Bubura flinched as a large foot prodded her, as if she were a crab that might be alive, not dead. Salt encrusted her gaping mouth and stung where the skin tore. Voices thudded hard around her like drums. Now arms grabbed hers and dragged her till she felt herself tugged onto her feet. The gold coral was torn from her neck.

She felt dazed, unsteady. As they pulled her, both legs seemed drained of strength. They sagged beneath her. Weakly, her head too light to hold high, she stumbled, and the light drenched her. Nei Bubura sank onto sand.

***

They had put her in a cage. The roots of a pandan tree had been tied together to trap her but the sun and breeze burst through the spaces between them. There was no room to stretch, or even stand. She bent her head down and held her knees.

Someone had heard her moving. Quick, light footsteps rained towards her. Pointing, their voices high, children giggled. Their dark hair glinted with salt and their skin was wet from the sea. One boy picked up a twig and pushing it between the gaps in her walls, prodded her below her neck.

A small boy was on haunches staring in at her with narrowed eyes. He reached in and pulled at her ear. The rest laughed loudly.

Nei Bubura's chest swelled with proud indignation. Lashing out with both arms, she beat against the roots but they did not snap. She only snagged her skin. Blood trickled free.

"I am the goddess Nei Bubura," she told them, her voice firm and steady though her heart felt wild.

Again they laughed. A handful of sand flew in her face. She spat and her raw eyes watered.

At a rasping yell the children ran. Nei Bubura breathed deeply, and waited. She heard the tread of a strong man, two. They were coming for her. But her gaze must show them she was not afraid.

One man gripped a knife, and wanted her to see it. Nei Bubura looked on it with dull disdain, and turned away, head high. With a sudden flick he sliced the root closest to her head. Through the opened space he pressed the sharpened coral blade between her breasts.

Nei Bubura glared, not at the knife but the man. Looking away, he withdrew. Then he threw his head forward and spat. As the spittle struck her scalp, they jeered. She felt it run warm and slow on her skin but she would not touch it. The sun would snatch it away.

Pulling a grotesque face, he rubbed his thick black hair, waggled his ears and lolled out his tongue. Nei Bubura did not understand the words he threw at her but she knew what they meant. She was not only different but less. Her bare head was so strange, so other, that it filled them with fear.

They were leaving now, but they would return. And they were too afraid to let her live.

***

In her dreams the coral bled. Running red, the island was a graveyard, a killing field. Along a flat rock path, a huge bird with no feathers rolled, whined and took flight. The sky was fiery and the earth roared. And all the men were dressed the same, walked the same, spoke with the same tongue and closed the same eyes.

Once again Nei Bubura shook herself free of sleep but still it held her in its power. She blinked and firmed her spine as upright as the cage allowed. Where were her grace, her strength and beauty now?

A breadfruit, sliced in half, lay just out of reach. A gift from a child, perhaps, who took pity on the strange bareheaded woman in her trap?

Taking the stick a crueller child had used to bait her, she leaned one arm out between the roots and stretched her muscles tight, tighter, until the twig touched the rough skin of the fruit, batted it, tipped it closer.

She smelt the man before his shadow muffled the sun. He picked up the fruit, one half in each hand, and dug in with his teeth, circling with his tongue. Nei Bubura turned away until she heard the fruit discarded on the sand. The man was shouting and beckoning. Others ran towards her.

The snapping roots were loud in her ears. Armed with knives, the men attacked the cage till it fell like firewood around her. But not for a minute did she think herself free. The voices made no music as they joined, competed, struck. Hands grabbed, but this time they raised her high, flat above their heads – like a body cold once the spirit had flown. Nei Bubura did not look up where the sun blazed but she heard the cries of the petrels and the urgent, bat-like flutter of their wings. Her head burned but she breathed in the breeze, the rain's freshness lingering on it. The fear was theirs, not hers. With her dignity she would make them understand.

She did not struggle as they tied her to a wild almond tree that spread white and pink against a sun-drained rock. When they snagged her flesh, leaving blood shining in beady droplets on green, she made no sound. Her dry mouth formed a smile as she gazed on the bright beauty of the flowers. In her imagination Nei Bubura crunched the sweetness of the hard fruit as if she believed the sight of it might sate her hunger.

A calling tern, swooping above the almond branches, speared over the water to dive. In her mind's eye Nei Bubura flew with the bird, out to sea and home.

Lashed to the trunk, her dress no longer stirring, she straightened her neck and felt her pride return. Their eyes on her bare head, their pointing fingers and jeering speech, could not diminish her.

Now they brandished knives and spears, only to curve them around her on the sand, a vicious necklace and a threat. But still she was not afraid. Smiling, she showed them love. In the silence that spread among them, and stilled the air, she felt a power that brightened her eyes.

Slowly they walked away. But the last of them, a boy who reminded her of Kakiaba, splashed her face with the rain caught in a coconut shell. Her heart surging, Nei Bubura blessed him with a murmur on glistening lips, and a nod of her cooled head.

***

Time had lost its shape and rhythms to the heat and hunger. The gift of water in the coconut shell had made Nei Bubura long for more, but sleep had made her forget. Now she woke to find the soft edges of darkness cloaking the rocks, sea and sky. From her scalp to the toes gritty with white sand, it chilled her skin. A flurry of breeze shook an almond from a branch but though she tried, bird-like, she could not catch it with an open mouth. Her tied wrists were torn.

Perhaps she would sleep again if she closed her eyes, until night was over. Nei Bubura told herself she must, or she would shiver unsheltered till her teeth chinked like the coconut shells in the storm. Maybe if she pictured the pools on her own island, bubbling to cool her sister's fever, the gladness and peace of her people would keep her warm as the night grew black and cold.

Soon, between sleep and waking, she glimpsed bats, eyes like black stars, wings scuffling. Above their dance, the moon began to peel open like a soft, ripe fruit. It heartened Nei Bubura with its gentleness and she bowed her head in thanks.

Through her weariness the waves began to chatter. A stirring, low. Had they come to kill her now? Stiffening, she would not crumple. Girl or goddess, she was Nei Bubura. She was different but she was not ashamed.

Something moved, quick and light. Not a crab or a rat. A tall shape, with breath that echoed her breath, warm on the night air.

As she felt herself untied, she thought she glimpsed the contours of a face she knew. The boy who reminded her of Kakiaba! He had slipped away to free her. But no! If he betrayed his people he would pay with suffering. Nei Bubura shook her head. She asked for no sacrifice.

"Nei Bubura," he whispered.

Kakiaba! The boy who loved her had come. Slowly she followed as he led her by the hand. Soft as two lizards, they stepped over the weapons towards the waves. In one hand he picked up a spear from the menacing chain, and sent it speeding towards the horizon. Then another. Two more, one in each hand, plunging gently into the waves. And again and again, light and sharp as rain.

Nei Bubura reached for his hand. Lightly, as if in a dream, she felt herself guided into the boat. His lips brushed hers. Sitting, she received a shell full of water, and as he began to paddle, she closed her eyes and drank.

Calm waves welcomed them out towards home. Nei Bubura heard nothing but the soft strike of the paddle through dark sea. She saw little but the white foam and the thin, smoke-grey outline of the boy who loved her. Remembering his kiss, she barely felt the touch of moonlight on her skin.

"Your queenly head is crowned in silver!" Kakiaba cried. "And I thought you were a girl after all."

"I am," she said, and laughed.

"I can't tell what you mean," he said, and she heard him smiling. "A goddess or a girl?"

Nei Bubura leaned her silvered head towards his and kissed his mouth.

"I am," she said.

The Goddess *is the postscript to* CRAZY DAISE, *a YA novel about alopecia.*

You can find out more about the authors* who have read and reviewed a story in this collection at the end of the book.

Sid's New Start is a tender portrayal of a man starting again when his marriage ends. It explores the assumptions we make when we meet people and empathically enters our dreams and expectations, and what we really long for underneath all that. Human, and humane.

Anne Hawkins, counsellor, Hertfordshire, UK

This is a witty story that will make you laugh out loud, but it's deep and sensitive too. A very enjoyable and satisfying read.

Billy Bob Buttons, author*, Sweden

Sid's New Start is clever and insightful, a modern fable with a twist in the tail.

John Marsh, retired civil servant, Doncaster UK

Sid's New Start *is another delightful collection of colourful characters with a gentle and amusing plot. This story offers an insight into the life of a newly divorced older man, and the possible options facing Sid all the way through make the ending all the more entertaining. Another master-piece from Sue Hampton.*

Heather Pretty, ex-school librarian, Northants, UK

I loved this sparkling, funny story. Sid finds that being cast off like a worn-out jumper, and forced to sell the family home, is a blessing in disguise – and I felt I was really inside his head and living in his world of greyness and no confidence.

Jill Hipson, BSL teacher, Herts UK

Sid's New Start was witty, warm and charming – and I didn't see the denouement coming! Sid's conversation with Jill on the phone was inspired – 'being happy is not as easy as it sounds'. So poignant and true! A delightful bedtime read.

Cindy Bodycombe, owner of Hollis Hill B and B, Broadwindsor, Dorset, UK

Sid's New Start

After Jill moved out in May, Sid found out how little belonged to him, and how much space was left behind. She'd chosen just about everything because he never minded much: blue or grey, stripes or spots, plain or wild, minimalist or baroque. It made no difference to Sid until he let it all go, along with her, and found himself rattling around between walls like a button in a shoe box. Out of place and a bit overwhelmed. Even the plants he'd come to regard with affectionate, fatherly interest in their progress were agreed to be hers, because she was the one who understood and met each one's individual needs. So without her, the only living thing in his home – not counting the odd woodlouse or spider – was Sid himself. And for a while he felt as if that life force of his was dimmed, or on standby.

He did consider a dog but that would require more energy than he seemed to be able to muster, and he'd always considered cats suspect: otherworldly and sleek with contempt. For a few months, Sid tried to keep the garden as Jill had loved it, but it was tiring and much too full of her – more than the house, which she had a tendency to neglect in order to spend her time with the flowers. After the picture of her carrying the final case down the drive, his most recurrent memory was of a wife on a floral kneeling pad with a trowel, her matching gloves caked with mud. That she'd abandoned the borders, in spite of that commitment and the dreamy look she used to wear when the roses bloomed, spoke volumes that weighed him down. That she'd ended the marriage just as he approached sixty-five and well-deserved retirement, was another shout he couldn't fail, in spite of hearing he now called "dodgy", to hear.

Sid had never seen himself as an imaginative man so perhaps it was no surprise that he hadn't foreseen the end of his marriage. No one else involved, he told people before they could suppose otherwise, although some of them seemed doubtful. It wasn't the chances of anyone hankering after Jill that seemed remote, not at all – but the chances of her doing anything so badly behaved, with or without a lover, as walking out on him. Even though she didn't go to church anymore, Jill had standards

and he'd struggled at times to meet them. She was particularly unequivo-
cal about the truth. His appeal, "Can't we say we've got flu?" on a
Saturday evening when he'd rather watch *Strictly* or *Casualty*, or anything
really, than go to a dinner party, would be met with, "I'm not lying. You
stay home if you prefer fake pixel people to real ones. Tell them. They
might understand."

It turned out, in the end, that all those friends were Jill's rather than
theirs, with the possible exception of Ted Newstead, who was married
to Jill's boss Venetia but whose interest in the newly-single Sid was as a
potential companion "out on the pull". And when it came to Ted, Sid
definitely preferred the telly. "Sorry, Ted," he told him when he called,
"but I'm a pixels man these days," and Ted seemed to take umbrage.
Either that or Venetia walked into the room.

Sid hadn't realised that being alone at sixty-five would make him feel
quite so pathetic. Or that in the first few days, like a teenager dumped by
some girl, he'd find himself sliding into squalor, with stubble sprouting
from his face and junk food delivered to his door by boys in leathers.
Their son Chris wasn't much support from Madrid, where he was living
with a Japanese girl. Sid couldn't see much point in Chris being depend-
ent on a so-called smartphone that could open jam jars, wipe his nose
and translate his lover's sweet talk if every time his old dad rang it went
straight to voicemail. Meanwhile, Cass was too stressed by a PhD in
something too inscrutably modern to remember, and nursing a grudge
against him for driving Jill away. Both of which, Sid decided, were equally
impossible for a mere man who scraped a third in his B.Sc to understand.

"No rush," Jill had said, about selling the house – as if as long as she
had detached herself from him, her objective was achieved, even though
she was only staying in a friend's spare room.

But after three weeks of inactivity of all kinds on his part, she put the
house on the market and called to inspect the place before viewers
arrived. He tidied up a bit and made sure he was at the library, reading all
the papers he normally swore about. When he returned he found the
garden watered and the place smelling of disinfectant, reinforcing the
inadequacy he'd been treating like a luxury. He was writing a text
intended to sound grateful and apologetic, but excused by "dodgy"
eyesight, when he discovered her note.

I've found a property. I'm sure you could do the same. She named some areas
where half the value of the four bedroomed semi-detached would pay for

a flat. Once he'd set aside a silently brooding kind of outrage, Sid decided the lethargy and humiliation needed to end so that something new and mysterious could begin. He bought the local paper and checked online. Soon he was obsessed by the idea of life, but not as he'd known it. He told himself he wasn't too old for possibilities and the vaguest were always the best.

It was September by the time the removal men came. No container-sized lorry required. Sid looked back at the house that had been home for thirty-two years, the home Cass was already mourning from a distance, and felt suddenly rudderless and in danger. Now the unknown seemed hostile territory, even after repeated viewings with little aim in mind except eliminating surprises. It wasn't a bad flat, and the lack of a garden to keep in order could be an advantage, but he wasn't sure that switching from a shoe box to a tea packet was much of an improvement for the average button. Which was how he liked to think of himself, generally: normal, and quite bright in his own way. But as he drove to pick up the keys to his new address he lost his inner shine remembering the neighbours, one below and one alongside. Ted might joke about a pair of apples within reach and ripe for plucking, but Sid wasn't sure he had enough conversation in him to maintain the most minimal of neighbourly relationships with two single women of a certain age, both of them welcoming, helpful and frankly alarming. Picturing the well-curled and glossed Louisa below him, and Hattie who could soon be smoking weed on the other side of his bedroom wall, he suspected they'd both have the kettle on already.

"Most of it gone to the wife then?" asked one half of his removals team some half hour later, with a box of breakables wedged under each thick arm.

"You renting?" asked the other, before he could reply, and when he said he'd bought the place the two of them exchanged expressions that could be called grimaces. "We get a lot of work here. Rapid turnover they call it."

"I call it Divorce Drive," called back the first, negotiating the narrow stairs through the open door.

The door to the left of it opened too and Louisa filled it, mainly with her hair. She slipped into open-toed heels and stepped out into the sunshine, shading her eyes.

"Morning!" she cried. "I've been known to work out even though I do prefer Pilates. Let me know if you lads need a hand. If not, I can brew up any time." The lads in question thought the time was now. She turned to Sid. "Greetings, neighbour!"

Her hand was cool. As he shook it, he thought he could smell that pear drop scent of fresh nail varnish. Her lips, toes and fingernails were all a shade he might have called tangerine before she caught him looking and said, "South Sea coral. Do you like it? Sugar?"

"Very nice," he said, "and I'm all right for tea just now, thanks."
She looked disappointed but said he could change his mind later and he noticed she didn't quite close the door behind her.

Careful not to trip over the filthy old sheet that trailed up through the flat like the train of a zombie bride, Sid entered his new home. Finding himself cornered at every move by "the lads" on their way up, down, around or through, he eventually made his way to the back window of the lounge and looked down on the shared green space he'd be paying through the nose to maintain. It was smoothly mown and glossy under a blue sky, with a couple of tables and benches, some flowers growing up the wall that hid the car park, and a few pathways to the flats at ninety degrees to his. He was thinking there were worse views when he noticed a woman on a bike working her way up the slope.

Recognising Hattie, in the kind of trousers they really did call pedal pushers, he wondered whether she was hurrying home for any particular reason. It didn't take her long to put the bike away and a few moments later she was striding down again. Taking off her baseball cap, she waved it at Sid. He held up a hand, noticing the thin plaits threaded through her straight, dark hair. The knee-length trousers were one startling multi-coloured print and her loose shirt another. On her feet were those chunky jelly sandals children wore; hers were lilac. With beads around her neck and one ankle, she looked like a festival-goer, tree hugger or folk singer, but nowhere near old enough to be retired. There was something girlish and uninhibited about her walk and her smile.

Stopping beneath his window, she grinned up.

"Hey, Sid!" she yelled, as if they'd grown up together.

He wondered what his world would have been like if he'd held her hand in the playground. Presumably he'd have an MI5 file after a lifetime of demonstrations.

"Come on in for coffee. I left some brownies cooling." Her voice was tuneful and light; she could get a job on Radio 3. Her hands bracketed her mouth for a stage whisper: "No hash today."

"Oh, thanks," he said, opening the window. Louisa could be overhearing every word. "But I'd better get physical, you know?" Instantly embarrassed, he imagined Jill's ridicule. The adjective had never fitted.

Hattie winked. "Good for you, Sid. Lou invited you into the palace, has she?"

"Well, I did decline in fact. Thank you. You're both very kind."

Sid retreated behind the closed window. The kitchen surfaces would probably benefit from a quick once-over. A few minutes later he heard two voices at the bottom of his stairs. Louisa's was deeper and smokier, outweighing Hattie's, but both were calling his name. It was a sting.

Soon he was in Louisa's spotless ground floor flat, along with a barefoot Hattie and a plateful of warm brownies she called legal: "Lou likes me to behave." Their crumbly texture and escapee nuts made him nervous on behalf of the hostess and the creamy suite which looked, but didn't smell, like leather. There he sat with his knees tightly joined, and as soon as Louisa disappeared to answer the phone, diligently retrieved with a damp finger whatever lodged between his legs. Hattie, who insisted on sitting on the floor like a student and licked her lips with abandon, seemed amused.

"I keep telling Louie she needs a cat – a white one, obviously. I suppose a pet rodent would do the job. They're very misunderstood, rats, and perfectly endearing if you can just shrug off conditioning." She winked. "Her heart's as big as her hair. Not the best hearing, though, so we can talk freely while she's projecting to the gallery up there."

Sid felt risk-averse just now but kept that to himself. "Have you been here long?"

"Four years for Lou, and I moved in six months later. Not sure who's corrupting who. She won't touch my home-brewed beer, though. Maybe I can tempt you, Sid."

Hattie turned a thin plait around two fingers. Sid thought she probably could, any way she chose, but he wasn't sure he'd survive. And besides, he couldn't imagine her bothering with him. He was sure there must be New Age or Greenie hunks with chests browned by all that bonding with Nature, guys who were more experienced in other kinds of connection than he'd ever be and knew how to make sex spiritual. Now she pointed excitedly out of the window to a bird she called a Long-tailed Tit. Sid realised, as she turned back to him, what she saw: a solid, round-faced, bland-featured pensioner with grey hair that thought it had been knitted and undone again, into thin, woolly kinks – and a chin that was trying to reproduce itself.

Hattie told him how lucky they both were, to be in full view of the nest box. "It was home to fledglings not so long ago. Exciting after years of dereliction."

Sid was struck by the thought that he'd lived through plenty of those in the office. He knew nothing about wildlife – another of his failings in Jill's book – but made the interested noises of the Lesser Spotted Urban Male.

"What did you do?" he asked her.

"Took pictures. Caught the mother feeding them."

She seemed to be searching for images on her phone but he explained: "I was really asking what you did for work. For a living?"

She put her phone away. He hoped he hadn't seemed heartless. "Ah. Carer."

"Oh. Rewarding, I imagine," he said. "Not financially, I dare say."

"Loved it. I only stopped because my favourite died. Fifteen years I pushed her wheelchair, bless her."

Sid thought he'd rather like to be cared for. That had never been Jill's style, not as far as he was concerned anyway. His either, but in the unlikely event of there being anything he could do for Hattie he'd be happy to oblige. The courgette brownies, which had seemed weird at first, had grown on him with their hint of chilli. He was accepting a third when, returning, Louisa declared that she did "like a man with an appetite".

"You're scaring Sid," Hattie told her.

"Oh I doubt it! Sid's a man of substance." Louisa giggled. "A rare species."

"Don't get the wrong impression, Sid," said Hattie, her voice lifting and falling. "We've been unimpressed by men thus far, but we don't hate them. Only a few of them anyway."

At which point, a loud knock on the door meant Sid was required. Both women offered to help him hang pictures – "I haven't got any" – and unpack breakables – "Nothing of that sort really." He left promising to invite them both back once he was straight. Left alone in his new home, he shook his head as he reran his own one-star performance. Positioning and sitting in the armchair he'd commandeered from the three piece suite, he noticed, against the backdrop of bare walls, new carpet and square boxes, how drab, worn and unsavoury it looked. It was an armchair that would be unintimidated by the crumbliest of chocolate brownies. And Sid told himself that when it came to his new neighbours he wasn't intimidated either.

Over the next couple of days he pretended to be busier than he was, and a few thuds and clangs backed up his alibi. But Louisa rang the doorbell to remind him the bin men came on Thursdays, and the recycling didn't allow for plastic bags but at Waitrose they made those into seats. On that occasion she was wearing some kind of jumpsuit and kitten heels but when he asked where she was off to, she said, "Oh, just my literature class. Do you read?" and Sid replied, "Not often." So she said, "More of a box set man, eh?" and laughed – even though personally he struggled to find the double entendre in that.

A while later, Hattie put a note through, written in shiny green: *As you may already have discovered, the walls are very thin so bang a fist on yours if the Arctic Monkeys are too loud. Ditto my snoring!* It was signed with an H and a single kiss. Not the kind of mail, he decided, that required a reply – especially as he'd heard her all right, or rather the persistent backbeat of something a fan would call 'driven'. He wondered how she snored, and the possibility that he'd find out at close hand one day raised his temperature. But he suspected Louisa would set lower standards in the emotional-psychological department. In her case, he'd need to buy a Kindle, download some lightweight American cop novel and switch to Jane Austen at her approach. Either way – lush Louisa or earthy Hattie – he must close the fitness gap.

Deterred by the cost of a golf club and the length of the waiting lists, he settled for jogging until the divorce settlement was finalised. Jill seemed to think he was the one being difficult, but he was better with money, always had been. His tenacity when he had to fight their financial corner used to earn him credit but now it made him "petty, frankly".

The fitness programme didn't last long. It was such a puffy, ruddy, sweaty and wobbly business, he'd have to do it in the dark or lose all credibility with his neighbours and himself. By comparison, Hattie frisked like a lamb and Louisa had all the sinuous stamina of a big cat (plus a dress that would provide excellent camouflage among leopards).

Sid came to the conclusion that he could give almost any club or class in town a miss without any sense of deprivation. The shelves he bought stayed in their packaging and the exotic pot plant he added to the trolley at the DIY store was drooping a week later. Then Cass came for the weekend, and examined each room, firing questions under the category of lifestyle.

"What are you, Ofsted?" he joked. "Do you need data?"

"Don't pretend you know anything about Ofsted. You never listened to Mum."

"Well, I don't know …" He might have, he supposed, now and then, but it was tiring, after a dull day with nothing to report, to be regaled with classroom drama. He hadn't questioned the way Jill came alive at work – sometimes to boiling point – and simmered down on the lowest of silent gases at home, with no characters and no narrative. Just him.

Next morning, Cass complained, having stayed in bed almost till afternoon, that the spare room was "male and unwelcoming". She seemed much more interested in her phone than his new world, and it was a bit galling when she got through to Chris, chatted, laughed and grinned as she moved around oblivious to his existence, and then handed over in time for her brother to say, "Hi Dad. How's it going? Can I call you back – gotta rush now."

But when she headed back to her studies after a pub lunch she murmured, with a surprisingly long hug, "Don't worry, you'll get used to it." Leaving him wondering what she meant. To the end of the marriage? A sex life that had slumped from sporadic to over? Reduced space and increased time? The washing machine and the many different verbs for cooking veg?

Cass had only been gone long enough for him to make a cuppa and slot in the next DVD in a box set from the mean streets of Chicago when he heard the doorbell. Hattie's hair was damp from the shower and she was wearing a sleeveless T-shirt that ended above her ankles. In spite of her thinness, he could tell the skin it clung to, along with the bones, wasn't smooth or tight.

"I saw your daughter go," she said, "and thought you might be in need of company."

He didn't deny it even though he didn't want to need anyone, not anymore. He hoped, when she said she could take the plant back for some rehab, there was no blame attached. They drank beer and she chose an old blues album from the Seventies, which she called her "heyday". She'd seen everyone, all the greats he admired most, including Hendrix at the Isle of Wight. And he had no idea why he'd missed them all. She asked about Cass and he didn't know as many answers as he should, but suddenly felt the loss of her. Of the little girl in unicorn pyjamas who liked him to read to her when he was around at bedtime – which wasn't often.

"Is she like her mum?" Hattie rearranged herself on the floor and hugged her knees a moment.

Sid supposed Cass would be feeding back to Jill right now, if she hadn't already. Or shouting at her for doing this to him, to "poor old Dad"? He couldn't be sure. Then he realised he hadn't answered the question.

"You didn't want the marriage to end?" she prompted, studying his face so intently that he wondered how feebly it sagged.

Then he cried. Only a little, just a dampness that burned and clouded. She held him and even though she was so small and slight, he felt lost in her, safe. Then he pulled away and said he was fine but he'd never thought about that before, not since Jill left.

"I suppose it's always easier to keep going," he said, producing a handkerchief that wouldn't be part of Ted's pulling kit. "I'm not one to analyse things, you know, pick them apart."

"I'm the opposite," she said. "I'll only take rockets and shooting stars. It's a serial kind of monogamy that way." The album ended and they debated what should follow. She sang along with Sandy Denny in the chorus and she sounded sweet to him. "Come to Glastonbury next year," she said. "Lou's allergic to mud but I'll look after you. I'm better with people than flats."

Sid smiled although he had only seen her hallway and the specked, grubby stairs leading up. She asked the time and said she'd better go; Louisa had made her a curry. As she carried the sick plant downstairs, he held back a risky comment about their unlikely friendship, and tried not to feel excluded when all he'd planned to eat was in a little foil container.

At the bottom she opened the door with one hand, leaned over the top of the plant and kissed his cheek. He wondered whether he might be falling in love but he couldn't remember enough to tell, apart from the arousal part, which seemed to be missing. He didn't need to be inside Hattie. It would be enough if she could see inside him, and didn't find fault with what she found.

The next day he cleaned the car, which meant a public appearance of a kind. He was creating quite a rivulet with his hose when Louisa came out with a basket of washing. Guiltily, Sid remembered the four whirly lines for some forty flats, positioned out of sight in the shade at the back of the garages. He hadn't done a wash yet but thought better of sniffing his armpits.

"I like a man with a hose," she said, making herself smile. Her mouth, which was wide and full, opened on teeth that one way or another must be expensive.

Most men over fifty would say she was kissable. But who was she, other than the sum of all the parts: the gym, the sexy Essex girl clothes, the Dynasty hair, literature class and lure of Drury Lane? She might have an I.Q. of a hundred and forty and a degree in medieval wall paintings for all he knew but that wouldn't make her real. People had to let go to make that possible and she looked to him like a woman who held on tight.

Still, either she liked him, or it was just a reflex. He'd have to watch her with the postman. For now it was her backside (he preferred the American "ass") that was hard not to watch as she swivelled away. Here he was, between two available women who would give his ego a quantum leap of a boost, either one, but no mammoth in a glacier could feel less capable of normal, hot-blooded male action of any kind. Shampooing the car was enough for one day; he was finding daytime antique shows quite addictive.

It was a shock and a disappointment when the female voice down the phone that evening was Jill's. She said they needed to talk and he said, "We did that bit. You talked already."

"All right," she said, "if you're going to be difficult, we'll skip the restaurant and I'll tell you now. I've met someone."

He let that settle. "You don't let the grass grow."

"I just wanted you to know that I'm moving in with him." She told him where: an expensive postcode. Sid felt a raging disbelief. How, given the amount of marking she had to contend with, had she pulled it off? "There isn't the time to take things slowly."

He asked none of the questions he was thinking. Instead she wanted to know what he was "getting up to", whether he was well, how it had gone with Cass. He was monosyllabic, presumably confirming her opinion that he was shut down, empty, nothing to give and no appetite even for taking.

"Sid," she said, after the silence had set, "we should have tried harder, both of us. Marriage isn't a Busy Lizzie." She waited again but he wasn't going to help her with that. "Low-maintenance, you know? Thrives whatever you do or don't. Can't we be friends?"

"I don't suppose so," he said. "Not really. Be happy. It's not as easy as it sounds."

Putting the phone down, he'd never felt so grey. He went to bed early, but next morning lay awake again much too soon, cold under the summer duvet and unsettled by a dream he couldn't remember. The sky was lightening but the road was quiet; he was getting used to the sound of a goods train, furred by distance but still a high-tech maraca. Just outside his door he heard a sharper rattle and keys landing. One of the two doors sandwiching his own closed, and he couldn't be sure which – until on the other side of his Ikea bedhead, a switch clicked on. His alarm clock, not yet relied on, showed five fifteen. Hattie had been out all night.

Either she'd been dancing in the woods with flowers circling her head, to celebrate some extra solstice he'd never discovered, or she had a lover. That meant rockets and shooting stars so he should be thankful it had been an away match, but Sid felt a new, acute loneliness. She might have mentioned the current status of that serial monogamy of hers and protected him from foolish hope.

In any case, he reflected, she was a rocker and a nymph too, with more spirit in her skinny left elbow than he could muster with thirteen undistinguished stone. Realism required a rethink and after all, Louisa was the kind of woman to make most men his age swell with pride to stand beside her. Maybe he should invite her to dinner in the hope that his spag bol would impress her more than it excited him three times a week. Perhaps just a cup of tea, with options like dandelion and tomato just in case, and expensive organic cookies free from anything she might have given up. Would wine be safer? It was probably more important, in fact, to add some personality with a few well-chosen pictures, and frames for photographs so that he didn't look suspiciously unloved. Flowers in a vase too; Jill used to have a way of just letting them go in water that seemed to work like a partnership deal.

He wasn't going to sleep now. Instead he poured himself some cereal and found a bad old American sitcom on TV. It felt like the day was half over when the clock showed nine, and with nothing established but an intention of finding one of those stores the size of the O2 that sold everything from tea strainers to bidets, Sid picked up his car keys and opened the front door.

"Hi!" Louisa was stepping out in yellow shorts with creases and turn-ups, white ankle socks and a silky black T-shirt. Greeting him, she fitted a cap onto her bouffant hair; it made her look like an American golf pro.

"We're off on a serious ride," she said. "Hat reckons we're looking at twenty-two miles there and back but that's the nearest stately home the National Trust can manage."

Sid echoed the distance. She remarked on his lack of a bicycle himself but that seemed neither here nor there. To join them he'd also need life support technology and a stretcher. He was making noises about getting fit when Hattie bundled out of the door to his left. In cut-off denims and a vest top, she bent to tie old trainers, presenting a backside that wouldn't look out of place on a schoolgirl.

"Hey, Sid," she said, looking up. "Sorry if I woke you too. I try to sneak around but I might as well be a heffalump."

"She means I kicked her out of bed for snoring," said Louisa.

As Sid continued to smile, she gave Hattie's rising backside the kind of playful slap that would guarantee him a harassment suit.

"Tart," said Hattie. "No kiss and tell round here."

Sid was still smiling, enjoying the show, when they linked hands. Louisa looked back at him.

"I've been told off for flirting but you did realise, didn't you? That we're a couple?"

Entertained and willing to play along, Sid kept up the smile, even though ...

"The odd and unlikely couple," added Hattie with a grin. They were walking just a step ahead of him, casually joined. No loosening of those hands.

A magpie showed blue in sunlight as it hopped away onto the green slope. The postman power-walking along from the furthest flat saw them and lifted one hand from his pile of mail. "Morning!"

"You're serious," said Sid.

"We are," said Hattie, and kissed Louisa's cheek. Sid remembered others like it, but since women kissed with such indiscriminate abandon, how was he to know? "We're even thinking about marriage. My first."

"All right," said Louisa. "My third." She smiled at Sid. "I saw the light in the end. No offence, Sid."

"None taken." He knew there had been clues; they just hadn't broken through his assumptions. "I'm happy for you."

Sid thought anyone living with shooting stars had better capture the moment in memory – the way he'd tried, another life ago, when Cass and Chris presented a birthday cake they'd decorated with forty-six candles and jumped like firecrackers in their pyjamas, even before the sugar rush, because they were happy for him.

"Poor Sid," said Louisa. "Nobody meant to lead you on."

Hattie gave her a sideways look at that. The three of them were approaching the garages where they'd mount bikes and leave him feeling ridiculous, his reason to buy cheap artworks snatched away.

"Have a nice day," said Louisa, in an American Southern States drawl.

"You'll find a good woman, Sid," Hattie told him.

"But why," he asked, "two homes when you could share one?"

Two heads turned. "Sid," said Louisa, "you've seen her flat."

Hattie rolled her eyes. "You've seen hers!"

He nodded. "Ah."

As they opened two adjacent garage doors, he wondered whether he'd learned enough from his years of agonising over Murray's serves and returns to join a tennis club.

Hattie was astride first. Louisa was wiping her saddle with a tissue. Sid hadn't managed to swing up his door.

"In weddings like ... it may not be appropriate, I dare say, but if you'd like a best man?"

"Sid," said Hattie, touched. "You softie."

"We'll let you know if you qualify," Louisa told him, fastening a helmet with wine-red trims that somehow accommodated her hair. "But don't worry, there's not a lot of competition."

Hattie led the way, freewheeling down the slope. Two left hands lifted in unison for goodbye, but they didn't turn. Sid was staring at his car and wondering whether anyone would phone the police if he beat it, Basil Fawlty-style, when his phone sang at him. Chris!

"Dad, sorry, it's been a bit mad here. How's it going?"

"Oh, you know, a bit mad. But I've made some friends."

You can find out more about the authors* who have read and reviewed a story in this collection at the end of the book.

Sky Lady *is a gentle and lyrical tale of a life that might have been, and of a song of dreams and wishful thinking. A genuinely charming story.*

Dawn Finch, author*, librarian and president of CILIP, Herts, UK

It is a small miracle that a character as affecting and complex as Eva's (in Sky Lady) *can be conjured in so few words. I feel I've known her all her life, which is decades longer than I've actually lived. She and her conjuror Sue Hampton will stay with me for a long time yet. What a treat!*

Matt Carmichael, English teacher and author*, Yorkshire, UK

Sky Lady *touches on a silence within, a very human story with dark corners and delicate mysteries to explore.*

Miriam Calleja, pharmacist, artist and author*, Malta

I loved Sky Lady. *The descriptions of the people and places were so good that I felt I was actually there and knew the characters. The story was gentle yet full of feelings that we all have when we reminisce, on landmark days, about life gone by.*

Heather Pretty, ex-school librarian, Northants, UK

A poignant reminder that as we change in both age and guise, our memories exist, unchanged and often growing in importance in the minds of friends; in the hearts of loved ones and acquaintances. A beautifully written story of how a briefly shared experience can lead to something unexpected many years later – hope for anyone who has daydreamed of being a muse ... or secretly yearned to rediscover one.

Neil Davies, teacher, writer and musician, Essex, UK

Such vivid imagery is created through Sue's magical descriptions between these short pages that Sky Lady *is as believable as if you were there. This short story puts you into the spin of Eva's life and relationships and before you know it, and suddenly you want to know everything.*

Thomasin Sayers, Community Flood Resilience Project Officer, Shropshire

Sky Lady

Eva had been aware, as the date approached, that her mother died in the hospice a few weeks before reaching this particular birthday. And after that, her dad's heart didn't bother to last another year. "Grateful": the word filled Eva's head, warming through the fuzz as she woke to early sunshine. And not just grateful to the hospice, although this particular Friday she was glad the other volunteers had ganged up to insist on covering her shift. She'd made it to seventy. Of course these days that was nothing; look at Helen Mirren, still what people called a sex bomb – although that was something Eva had never been, thank God. Life had always had enough challenges.

In a carefully worded email, sent to everyone she truly loved or liked very thoroughly, she'd given notice weeks earlier of the way she wanted to celebrate. The schedule began with breakfast on offer from eight till ten, ideally in her little garden. Of the four possible guests, two were definitely the remote kind. But she'd better get cracking. Not that she was offering eggs these days. *This will be vegan,* she'd pointed out in italics – scaring off a few. Whatever people chose to do, Eva hoped they'd come out of love or not at all, and compliantly minus gifts. Her wording had expressed regret for too much consuming and a desire – also a need – to tread lightly on the earth. Rising from bed, she pulled up the blind and looked down on the staple-shaped border rimming the fence. The last roses were shedding but the sweet peas were at their delicate best, their fragrance just as heady.

Eva showered, more aware than usual of her body at seventy. It would never flaunt a bikini again, or anything designed for strutting or swanking. Since the surgery she'd been glad to be intact and functional, if reconstructed inside. The scar had left her abdomen swollen, snatching and tugging at the smoothness she'd rather liked between her hipbones. Still, she'd embraced it in the end. It was the only way. But she hadn't forgotten the helplessness or the pain that mattered too. That was learning; it was human. And hope was finding the magic in the now.

"Grandma," Manda asked in spring, when they drank Prosecco togeth-er to mark Manda's twenty-fourth and a couple of glasses made Eva ridiculous, "how long have you been on your own now?" And Eva laughed out loud. Not because the answer was thirty-three years – since Micky left for university, only ever dropping by after that – but because Manda was really asking about what was called her 'love life', and there was oh, so little to say. But the memory of sharing it made Eva vaguely uncomfortable, especially given the reaction from a granddaughter who was not only sober but already more experienced in a notches-on-the-bedpost sense. For Eva, a little alcohol after months without a drop had been way too much. And she rather feared Manda would have told her friends. It was probably all over Facebook by now!

Eva dried herself mindfully, because this flesh of hers was old and entitled to tenderness and the spirit inside was, of course, whole decades younger and freer. She wouldn't see Manda until the ballet but as the landline rang she knew it would be her, from the commuter train to London. Eva let the towel fall and hurried naked across to the living room, forgetting the curtains she didn't draw on summer nights. Ah well.

The phone named *Dear Manda*.

"Happy Birthday to you ..." Manda sang all four lines. She had rather a pretty voice, but that might be "granny thinking". That was what Manda called it when Eva told her how beautiful she looked, or how clever she was with technology. But she was Grandma really, and that was probably the best role she'd filled. Fewer mistakes, no tension or blame, and no part to play, in fact, but her real self – minus the details withheld, until the Prosecco.

"Thank you, darling. Are you on the way to work?"

"Yeah. Got a seat for a change. Who's coming to birthday breakfast? Tim? Or is he already there?"

"I won't dignify the postscript with an answer," she said, smiling. "We'll see."

"I hope Dad's called?"

"Well, not yet." Micky did things in his own good time, and that was fine. "You're the first."

Manda sounded pleased about that. She said she'd better go but she'd see her at Sadler's Wells and Dad had better not be late. "I've got you a well-timed birthday surprise and don't tell me off because I had to buy it. And art doesn't count as like … consumption. Is that a disease?"

Eva said it was, yes and yes. She was a little dubious about Manda's taste in art but thanked her anyway and said how lovely it would be to see her again. Manda hoped Prosecco would be involved and Eva warned her that if there was any chance of that, she'd acquire a headache and take to her bed instead – which made Manda laugh disconcertingly.

Eva wished she could remember exactly what she'd told her that night about the lecturer who was her grandfather in a technical sense only, and might be dead. Not forgetting an almost-husband who wanted, for six whole months in the early Eighties, to make up for all that and be a father to Micky, but had no idea how. And Tim, who had been her second-best friend for so very long that it was strange, and disloyal as well as natural, to consider the possibility she must have worded for Manda somehow, betraying thoughts she'd hardly tracked. She had a feeling she'd even mentioned the lodger who went on to be Ash Golden but had a regular name then, his own.

Eva had only just put down the phone and tied on her faded cotton kimono when it rang again. On the tiny screen she still hadn't deleted Dee from *Dee and Tim*.

"Tim," she cried as he greeted her, thankfully without a tune. "Bless you!"

Tim said he didn't need to ask how it felt to be seventy because he'd got there a few months before her. Eva remembered his twentieth, shared with Dee who was five days ahead of him, and the pair of them moving as one eight-legged, psychedelic being: hippies before the rest of the college caught up. "I'm pregnant," she'd told Dee that night in the Ladies, adding the truth she never shared with her parents when they dragged her home but couldn't break down her claim not to know who was "responsible".

"Your *Art lecturer?*" Manda had echoed almost fifty years later over the bubbly.

"And personal tutor, yes," she admitted. "Married and forty, and a serial philanderer. But I didn't know that then. I didn't know anything much at all."

Tim had been angry at twenty, determined to get "the lech" sacked. Now, on the phone, he was sad: "I want to say love from both of us. The reality still feels unreal. And I can't make you a cake like hers." He

105

stopped as she mm-ed. "Sorry, Eva. It's a happy day, yours."

"Yes," she told him, a little concerned about the ongoing presence of Dee – or at least, the way he framed it, more Spiritualist than Quaker. But then one reason the three of them sat in silence at Meeting on Sundays was that words were so inadequate. Never more so than with death, and there were days when she didn't believe in Dee's either. But at that other birthday party long ago, the pair of them believed in her – while her parents lost all faith. Tim was a good man, the best. "But you're allowed to be honest after all these years," she told him, "whatever the date says."

Tim thanked her and said he'd see her in the woods for lunch. "I can't promise to dance, though. Arms might manage a swirl or two but the legs wouldn't know how to join in."

Another reason for gratitude, thought Eva: no arthritis to stop her dancing. She couldn't help its effect on that Art lecturer when she was just a girl and it was wilder than she was, less inhibited. And the hair, now tucking under her ears, had its own choreography.

Was she relieved that two years after losing Dee, Tim felt half of a couple still?

Waiting for the kettle to boil, Eva was checking her fridge for mush-rooms, tomatoes and the vegan patties she'd improvised the day before – as if her memory, sometimes unreliable, might only be imagining their readiness – when the phone surprised her yet again. Surely not Micky, unless Manda had demanded action?

"Grandma! Turn the telly on. BBC1. I've just had a tip-off. Run!"

"Tip-off?"

"From Jav. Go, Grandma! Bye!"

"Manda …" But she'd gone. Jav was the new boyfriend but she hadn't met him yet and she couldn't imagine what on earth he could mean.

Standing back from the heavy little box of a set everyone urged her to replace, Eva recognised the voice first, even with the American overlay that had thickened with the years. She wondered whether Ash Golden might have had something they called 'work' done to his face. His hair, skimming his shoulders now, faked the same old lustrous black; his skin appeared stretched as well as tanned. Lounging on the studio sofa in a caramel shirt and white jeans, he looked cooler than his music had been for a very long time.

"Yeah," he told the presenter, with what they used to call "his trade-mark twinkle", "I guess we all reach an age when we look back. And the past is elusive but powerful anyway."

The presenter was half his age. Eva was sure she must have asked the producer, "Ash who?" because he'd been off-screen most of the century.

"But what we all wonder of course is whether these ladies are fictional, like characters in a novel, or real …"

"Sure, yeah." He twinkled. The teeth were suspiciously good. "The creative process blends the two, you know, and blurs the difference. And you have to remember that the memory's kinda shot anyway."

"So there may or may not have been an older lady in an embroidered sky-blue kaftan?"

Kaftan … It took Eva a moment, as Ash opened his hands, shrugged and offered up another smile. "Hey, who can say for sure?"

"So let's hear a taster of *Sky Lady* from the new album, *Encounters of a Tender Kind*, released today. Ash Golden, thank you and welcome back."

Sky-blue … Now the predictable chords in a familiar order were schmaltzing and thumping through her living room, plus violins and minor angst and a soft-focus Ash walking with wind in his hair through a London street. Eva stood, remote control in hand, tempted to end it now but unable to press the button just yet.

"*Landlady, sky lady, blue kaftan high lady.*" Such a beautiful garment, from the Kings Road, a stupid extravagance, a vanity. "*You were gentle, you were kind and you're still on my mind. Landlady, sky lady, Mama you could fly lady.*" On her screen a kaftan not unlike it lay creased on a bedroom floor beside some slippers she would never have worn, and discarded jeans. A guitar leaned against the wall behind.

So much more than enough! Eva blanked the screen. The silence had a welcome tang after the artificial sweetener masquerading as music. Already she could picture Manda's elation, greeting her in the theatre bar: "Sky Lady!" But how was Micky supposed to react? At fourteen he'd idolised the strumming lodger; she'd worried he'd take advantage of pot on the premises – and couldn't be sure he never did, in spite of the rules she tried to lay down. 1980, spring through summer. What had it been – four months, five? But there'd been no flying of the bedroom kind … had there? Could she have deleted it along with other misdemeanours that didn't fit with the mama she was then or the Quaker she'd become?

"Mum," Micky had said to her just recently, mid work-talk of some kind, "I told you this last time I called." As if with no idea that people her age had to live with the fear of dementia, Alzheimer's, the orange brain minus most of its segments. Something stopped her apologising. But in fact, he was equally forgetful of the details he hardly heard however carefully she worded them, while she, as listener, animated all his living news with colour and sound. It had been more painful that way, with his divorce, but it was all she could do, with him never still and always frantic about it.

She couldn't have forgotten sleeping with Ash Golden, even if he hadn't, for a while, morphed into a global superstar – abandoning in the process the boyish musical energy that made him so attractive in his forward, open, available way.

"In my version, miladdo," she announced in the empty room, "I turned you down."

It wouldn't suit him to remember that. She'd only smoked his "waccy baccy" once, out of curiosity and to amuse him because he saw her as respectable. Meditation wasn't only safer; it led her further, deeper, beyond. But memory was a network of paths that only took her so far. Every search ended in a haze of images washed with feeling, but few sequences to track.

"How old are you?" she believed she asked him, as he moved in more equipment than she'd accumulated in thirty-four years. Probably wondering why she'd agreed to a lodger at all, just because his godmother lived next to Dee and Tim.

"Twenty," he said. "Nearly."

Chimes like that never stopped. The same age she'd been when an older man had done to her what college life allowed him to do. That was history she was hardly likely to invert and repeat, not even as some kind of psychotic revenge on men. And if her memory of Ash was to be trusted, he would in any case have strolled away and left the hurt to her.

She hadn't forgotten how thin he was, and pretty. And charming, too, in spite of the dope and disappearances.

"I wrote a song," he said one evening. "Will you tell me what you think?"

And she'd liked it, because it was whimsical, off-centre, a surprise with a shift of gear that must have rocked the neighbours out of their complacency. So it made her sad that now he was plugging some financial deficit with something so bland and manipulative.

He'd seemed happy then.

Ash Golden was in the back of the Merc, which had only moved half a mile out of the studios in crazy traffic, when Shirelle took a call, peppering it with slow, uncertain sounds like, "O ... K," and "Yeeaaah?" against the soundtrack of the new album in his ears – until she said, "I'll check with Ash and call you right back."

He cut the feed. "Another interview?"

Shirelle was half his age but she'd struggled with the early start and he wondered how much booze she'd downed last night. Her hair was flagging and her skin was blotchy.

"The studio took a call from some guy called Jav who knows your landlady. Sky Lady. Well, his girlfriend does, because she's like her ... grandma?"

Ash wished she wouldn't turn information into a question he couldn't answer. But he should have known this would happen: the first of any number of crazy calls.

"If they want to make a story of it, that's their business." Shirelle looked fazed. "But she's classy. If she's still alive."

"You don't know her name?"

"No, I don't," he told her, though he might have hoped she'd pay attention to the interview. "I know her son's first name. Let me talk to them."

Micky, it was – like Dolenz. Ash's sister had been a Monkees fan when he was a toddler; the lyrics of their hits had set firmer in his brain than *The Farmer's In His Den*. Strange how things stuck. If any callers wanted to take his time they'd have to know that. And if it all went pear-shaped and Sky Lady had dementia or a book deal, he'd have words with Cy about creative sales strategies and human brand regeneration.

Breathing deeply, Eva settled herself as if in Meeting – or tried, but unsuccessfully, because what she felt was outrage – inasmuch as she allowed herself that for personal (rather than global justice) reasons, because understanding was so much more helpful. She felt wronged. Whether he'd genuinely convinced himself that he made expert and beautiful love to her – and she suspected that was what it would have been, given the advanced level of his confidence and experience – or used decades and drugs as an excuse for speculative fiction, he was marketing a lie. And a kiss-and-tell story was so much more thrillingly believable in a tabloid age of suspicion than the dull old truth of restraint, of abstinence.

All right. Eva extended her back on the kitchen chair. She'd been avoiding reactiveness of this kind for decades now. And she must remember everything she knew for sure and cherished, find God in everyone. Whatever she'd been to him then, he meant her no harm. And she was sorry for what he'd lost.

Drinking coffee, inhaling it, she reminded herself she was happy and grateful.

But he'd identified her. Although it must be admitted that she'd aided and abetted him in that, with Prosecco freedom. Until Manda's girl-birthday, the only living keeper of that secret, such as it was, had been Tim. That she'd fancied her lodger more than reason should have allowed. That they'd kissed – just the one time, but in that way that seems endless …

Doubtless his celebrity status would prevent anyone crediting her denial should she expose herself with such a thing. Which of course she had no intention of doing. She had only taken a couple of sips from the coffee when the phone rang.

"Mum, this is some birthday surprise," Micky began. "Did you have to?"

"Thank you for ringing," she said, looking out to the garden and up at the cloud trying to overwhelm the sun. "I'm hoping for a lovely birthday."

"I don't normally watch breakfast TV …"

"I'm glad you're having a more relaxed start …"

"Manda rang. I caught the song, if you can call such crap music …"

"Oh, we agree on that. Micky, I …"

"He was only a few years younger than me, for fuck's sake!"

Eva held the phone away, arm straight. She'd never reached immunity from the word and still winced when it came from family. That way she could barely hear as he continued. When a pause was followed by "Mum?" she brought it back.

"My memory of events is very different from Ash Golden's, Micky. Mine tells me I was never his lover and I believe it. You can take your choice."

His silence seemed positive until he said, "It makes no difference. Everyone will believe him."

"Everyone? Because the whole world knows I had a sky-blue kaftan?"

"No. I'd forgotten that. But I tell people – that he was our lodger. Of course I do, who wouldn't?"

"I haven't!"

"I wonder why! Look, Mum, I know it's your birthday but I'm reeling here, all right?"

"Not really, because …"

"I have to work now so let's leave it, yeah?"

She wished he wouldn't talk like a teenager. It was a shame he had to call at all, a shame he didn't trust his own apparently razor-sharp faculties to point him towards truth as opposed to fantasy.

"By all means," she said.

With an out-breath of exasperation, he ended the call. Eva remembered that he hated her "being patronising", or treating him "like one of your special needs knitters" – never having learned much respect for textiles.

More breathing required. The sun warmed her face as she returned the phone to its handset. If no one was coming to breakfast, perhaps she would sauté herself some mushrooms and make some toast.

Micky *told people*. So, since spring, had Manda – told her friends, her mother no doubt, and her Jav. It seemed Eva's only sanctuary from a knowing but misinformed world would be Meeting. She'd be surprised if three out of ten Quakers would recognise Ash Golden if he passed them in the street. And of those, not even Luella would whip out a phone.

A sound from the hallway turned out to be the post, not a guest. Eva left the mushrooms on a low flame, savouring one of her favourite smells as she retrieved a little pile of cards. She was good at handwriting, identifying Manda's because of the heart replacing the o in Thorne, Luella's stylish flourishes (she was the most likely of those three Quakers to denounce Ash Golden's artistic decline) and octogenarian Abida's evenly sized print. She'd hoped Luella would drive Abida and her walking stick to breakfast, but it seemed she was eating alone – and why not, for goodness' sake? There was no need whatsoever to feel unloved – especially now the world apparently believed her loved and lost by a pop star old enough to be labelled a 'legend'!

Breakfast was a gift. Eva ate slowly, mindful of textures and flavours, the sounds in her mouth of the slippery mushroom crescents and the crispness of crust. Once, she had lost her appetite for all this – not when Ash left, as he was always sure to do, but when the next man to move in couldn't rescue her with a ring or be a father without rage.

Brought up at cool, low volume, Eva had ever since felt battered by shouting, banged doors, thudding fists, grabbing hands. Micky knew that, if he knew her at all. And he'd find softness again; she'd raised him in its cradle.

Breakfast finished, Eva prepared the picnic, which would fit snugly in her bike basket. Then she washed up, stood the cards on the windowsill and realised she wasn't technically dressed. In the absence of that sky-blue kaftan, she chose something almost as comfortable, a charity shop find in primary colours that fell loose from her never-very-ample bust. She had a photo of him, not in an album for family and close friends but a boot box. Why not, since her memory needed back-up?

When she stood on the bed and reached for it on top of the wardrobe, the lack of dust surprised her. Lifting the lid she found Ash Golden tilted at the tip of the haphazard pile, waiting: smiling, with a cigarette that looked legal between his fingers, casual outside the front door with yellow roses behind. Because she'd shown Manda that night! Of course she had. The pair of them had delved, scattering pictures until they found him. Manda had been incredulous that the has-been had once been "hot".

"You could sell that to the Press Association for four figures," she told her.

"Oh, I'll leave it to you in my will," she'd answered – or the Prosecco had – when she should have reminded Manda that the media and celebrity culture missed the point of everything, didn't understand value without numbers.

Now she carried the box of photos to the kitchen table. If this wasn't a suitable day to rummage, sober, through her life, she didn't know what was.

Not yet out of the city traffic, Ash swore, laughed and swore again. So it was her, Micky's mother. Eva Thorne – and he should have remembered the surname too because of the rose bushes by the front door, and her not being spiky at all but fragrant too. But that was the distant past; now she was an OAP, a spinster. She could make him look even older than he felt.

"Ambushed," he'd told Cy. It was all very well for agents and record labels to talk human interest, but this felt unnerving. And all it took was a blue kaftan when they could have used a red one, let the frauds bundle in, and leave it to the press to give their fantasies an airing while he kept smiling and shrugging and blaming some kind of purple haze.

Just one Sky Lady would take him nowhere he wanted to go. And Cy was seriously excited, but that was a permanent condition with agents and Ash sometimes longed to find an instant cure.

"She wasn't a pushover, man," he pointed out.

"What do you mean?"

"She was independent-minded."

"I thought you didn't remember her name!"

"It's coming back, all right? I just don't know what her story will be."

It was all good, Cy insisted, whatever – even if she portrayed him as a dope-head more sexed-up than a Bonobo. Especially if …

Ash needed a face, eyes, hair, something besides the kaftan. But he didn't suppose he could pick her from a line-up of old Eighties photos, never mind a pension queue at the Post Office. To write the song he'd thrown together an identikit sketch in his head, like a police artist with a suspect, but now it got in the way. Out of touch with reality again: the story of his life.

"And you're sure she's not going to have me leading a singalong in a nursing home?"

Cy said the granddaughter's boyfriend hadn't met Eva Thorne but believed she was in good shape, mentally as well as physically. Like Ash should have known she would be.

But was that bound to be a good thing? He had a feeling he should have chosen a different track for the single.

"All right," he said, tired now. "But we stay in control, yeah?"

"Always," said Cy. "You're the story, not her. But the big birthday – on release date, for fuck's sake – has to be a shit-hot opportunity …"

"Come again?" Ash guessed he must have lost that bit to a siren.

"*Sky Lady's* **Golden** *Birthday,* right?" Cy continued. "We send a shitload of flowers and get photos. She's overwhelmed. Armfuls of them hide her saggy tits but her eyes are full too. Why wouldn't they be?"

"Cy, you're making me sick, man, all right?" Ash passed the phone to Shirelle. He needed music. Were they playing it yet? Ignoring what he could hear of Cy bullying Shirelle, he searched radio stations … and there it was, the hook everyone would be singing by the weekend. Cy fixed everything.

Eva left the photo of Ash Golden at the peak of her past, some of it black and white but oddly stirring, never more so: people she'd cared for, places she couldn't restore because they'd vanished now, and the impossible, heady truth of a life, just a small one. She fitted the lid and carried the box back to her bedroom. Checking the clock beside her bed, she was startled to find so little of the morning left. But through the glass the sun felt warmer now; the woods would be glorious.

The phone! She hurried, hoping it might be Micky. She didn't need an apology, just understanding and a little credit.

"Grandma, don't be angry with Jav. I already have been. He called the TV studio because he thought it'd be lovely if Ash Golden wished you happy birthday …"

"Oh, darling, please don't tell them where I am. I'm much too old for that kind of surprise. My heart might not withstand it."

"Don't say that! I'm so angry with Jav but he doesn't know you, what you're like …"

"A private person, darling. Not a lonely old girl who needs a rock god to reach down from the clouds of celebrity and pat my head."

"I know! I said so. I might have to dump him."

"Oh, not on my account, please. It's just a very bad song."

She told Manda not to worry, or overreact either. "I'm having a lovely birthday," she added, trying not to qualify that with the thought that just for once she'd been hoping not to let the world break in, wielding every kind of power she didn't rate or need. "I'm off to the woods. I'll give your love to the teddy bears."

Of course a girl of Manda's generation would simply think that barmy. Eva checked her mental leaving-the-bungalow list and wheeled the bike out from the hallway into sunshine.

How beautiful.

Through the calls Ash noticed Cy's smile didn't narrow. Still *all good,* apparently, and it was years since he'd had attention like this. Nostalgia sells. The vid didn't have to be a Tardis back to that particular street he couldn't picture because it whizzed people back to their own past, when life seemed free as love. Three more interviews lined up, and counting. Cy said he could work out a line on Sky Lady and hold it: respectful, tender, vague.

The more he thought about Eva Thorne, the less he was certain of anything. There was no husband around, for sure, but if she was the confiding type he'd heard plenty more stories since to displace hers and sometimes he felt like his head was almost out of space. That could be a lyric once he settled for cruise liners.

He had no clue what she'd say but he'd made her look good, hadn't he? Most women would be grateful.

The hush as Eva reached the woods was striking; it felt like an entrance and a departure. No barking, no children, and little wind to orchestrate the trees. Eva came at least twice a week, to get her own exercise as well as to breathe the green air and find the light in it, however cool or dim. Today the sun felt soft through the leaves, but energising too. There was always hope and nature restored it. Other Quakers said they couldn't cycle and 'be' in a prayerful or meditative sense, not at the same time, but Eva could, with more trees than traffic. She just felt the life around her, and her part in it.

A woodpecker rattled a greeting. This silence was so full, it made Eva feel more than satisfied, not only glad but replete. She remembered, leaning her bike against the trunk of a beautiful beech, how much Manda used to love being here too, as a tousled child who needed to run. It was good to lift off the helmet she'd had to promise, after six decades on wheels, to wear – and feel the breeze break up her flattened hair. *Peace,* she thought, letting the air fill her lungs and the sun toast the back of her neck. How blessed she was to know its meaning.

Looking up, she saw Luella's car sneaking up – and an arm waving out of an open window. She had good friends. And none of them would have watched a TV chat with a faded rocker, or played Radio One in the car.

Luella parked in a dusty space under a tree and helped Abida out, stick first. Eva went to welcome them with hugs, glad they seemed to have respected and understood her words about things. They had only just settled Abida at the picnic table when she recognised Tim's electric car. Luella was very impressed, although she suggested they should fit solar panels on top.

"I'm sorry if this is breaking the rules," he said, emerging with a small bunch of roses, "but flowers cannot be described as stuff."

"Oh, Tim! How kind." Eva thanked him, kissed both cheeks and smelt the roses. They were yellow.

Smiling up close to the scent, she was sure Tim wouldn't remember enough to make that connection. He and Dee had visited her wherever she'd been, including the old terrace in NW7 where everything leaked so a lodger's rent helped to fund repairs, and an overnight stay meant bringing their own sleeping bags. But she didn't suppose he'd remember the lodger's stage name, never mind the one he'd been born with – or the backdrop to the Polaroid that would have trapped him forever without celebrity. And its complications. She would have liked to spare the twenty-year-old all that.

Lunch was good, and conversation summery, reflective. Eva didn't need to be centre-stage and liked listening. Luella and Abida considered her a youngster so no one asked chat show questions about numbers but Tim took some "birthday photographs" and promised he hadn't joined Facebook. And Eva was glad she'd thought to turn off her phone.

"There must be lots we don't know about each other," said Luella, picking cress from her teeth. "From all these weeks, hours and minutes we've clocked up between us. I think that's rather thrilling. And I like being mysterious."

Abida put down her apple juice with a shaky hand and said she hadn't noticed. "Eva's the closed book."

Eva could have said it was a slim volume, or that one day she'd dip in and share a paragraph from an early chapter they didn't see coming. But she chose silence and a smile.

Tim left first, wishing her a great night at the ballet, and Eva thought better of telling him to be on standby in case Micky stood her up. She waved both cars away and mounted the bike, setting the flowers carefully in the basket and leaving her phone pleasingly dead. Slowly riding home, she glimpsed a solo deer not far from the roadside, and stopped off for a close encounter. It was young, holding its head high and still as its eyes fixed on hers. And for a moment nothing moved, as if time had stopped, her seventieth birthday would never end, no leaf would ever fall again, and the sun would hold everything safe and bright forever. Then, smiling, she took a step backwards and the deer broke away. A squirrel landed a foot from her feet. A car ground past, and overhead a faint whine drew her eyes to a sky where white began to streak into blue.

She saw the black car parked outside the bungalow but couldn't place it, vehicles not being her forte. Maybe Micky had changed his again? He'd be cross with her for "radio silence" but she hoped they could leave the last call behind. As she pedalled closer, someone stepped out and stood facing her, holding something small but not waving or smiling. No one she recognised, and not dressed like a delivery man but suited, slick. She drew close enough to see the sweat on his forehead.

"Hello," she said. "Can I help you?"

"Eva Thorne?" Without waiting for a reply – which she decided not to give – he reached onto the back seat while she stood, holding the handlebars.

She thought at first that the upholstery was some kind of gorgeous, buttery velvet – until it dissolved and all she could see, and smell, was roses – a bouquet so big and wide it blotted out the man in black and most of the vehicle too. It was disarming, intoxicating.

"Happy birthday from Ash Golden," muttered the male voice, and she might have laid down her bike and reached out, instinctively, for the yellow roses to dwarf the bunch in her basket, to fill the bungalow, every vase and room. But another voice, female this time, spoke her name as she sprang out of the passenger seat where Eva hadn't even seen her, with a camera to catch her as she received her gift.

"Take them to the hospice, please. Thank you." Eva reached instead for a card she kept in her purse, with the address on it, and managed to shield her face with the other hand. "It's only half a mile away. Left at the junction, first right. Please. You get to make the rules on your seventieth

117

birthday and that's mine."

Leaving the man with arms full of flowers, she picked up her bike and walked it to her door, careful not to turn her head. The girl was behind her, calling, "Eva! Is it true you're the Sky Lady?"

"Oh, I'm not sure it's truth you want," she said, quietly, "but I have my own if Ash would like to hear it himself another time. Please, deliver the flowers now before they fade. I promise they'll be loved."

She turned, and hoped her face told them something they could read. The girl turned too, towards the road. Eva waited for her to reach the car before she unlocked her door and wheeled the bike inside, closing it behind her. The bungalow pricked with thick, baked-in heat, so she opened the windows. There was a little vase Tim's buds would fit perfectly.

No buzz from her landline. Not that it mattered, or could change a single note in the music inside her, when the dance began or the journey or the twilight, but he'd never call.

You can find out more about the authors* who have read and reviewed a story in this collection at the end of the book.

Included is a beautifully nuanced story of love and loss, compassion and courage. It chronicles how life breaks a couple's hearts and then offers them an unexpected opportunity for solace. The writing is, without exception, clear as a deep mountain stream, rich with meaning, and never sentimental.

Robin Gregory, author*, USA

Included is a lovely, haunting and often melodic little story about loss, heartache and acceptance.

Andy Frankham-Allen, author * and editor, Cardiff, Wales

Included is a sensitive and well-written, yet slightly eerie and uncomfortable tale, of both rejection and acceptance, leading us perhaps to question our long-held moral and ethical values. It is sensually evocative of the '70s, examining love, loss, forgiveness and adjustment, drawing us into a mysterious web of 'innocent' deceit, yet leaving us with a sense of poetic - if not traditional — justice.

Mary Biddington, teaching assistant, Cheshire

Included is a daring story about grief and the healing power of love. While the theme is familiar, Sue Hampton bravely tackles controversial gender issues and the notion that sometimes we find our real families rather than just being born into them.

Cimberli Banton, writer and artist, USA

I loved this story, which is moving without being sentimental. I liked the imagery and the way the author lets the reader fill in some of the gaps.

Lisa Emery, Reason Bookshop and Café, Watford, UK

Included

Everything else has transformed over time, even Slough. But the old songs are intact in the storage facility. There was one, after Adam died, that I knew I shouldn't play when I was alone, but I used to put the LP on the deck, and sit and shake. *Without You* from *Nilsson Schmilsson*: an enormous hit from the year my boy started school. Between simmering verses, there's a chorus where the loss bursts its lid. That track was how we were, together in the house, the car, the town. We talked the verses, muted and beaten – while inside, the chorus kept roaring.

When I said I wanted to move, John didn't see the need.

"We won't leave it behind," he said.

I knew *it* meant *him*. John was finding the name hard to say. "Adam will be with us wherever we go," I told him. "How could we bear anything else?"

I looked at my husband and hoped I could carry on loving him. Grief is like surgery. Things had been chopped and reconnected inside him and it showed in his face, the way he held himself, walked, breathed at night. His smiles were like missed notes, falling short. I saw – I heard – his attempts at normality slip away into a void and that was where he'd find me, in mine. That chorus was wild in the silence as we held each other.

Adam held us together in a way, and I didn't want that to end. But not in the house where we'd brought our baby home from hospital. Where our boy had sat at the supper table and said, "I don't feel well." Where I'd found him on the bathroom floor, clammy through pyjamas.

"Please, John. I can't stay here."

So the house went on the market and I threw myself into the search for something just far enough away to mean a different school uniform, park and supermarket. Somewhere I wouldn't bump into the other mums – who nearly cried at the sight of me, and the Angel Delight and Nesquik missing from my trolley. The next Friday evening, mainly because *Prox-*

imity to Burnham Beeches sounded good to me, we went to view a property fifteen minutes away in John's new Cortina. He played Olivia Newton John all the way there, and looking at my reflection in the passenger window I felt old at thirty-six, my hair flat and my face empty.

John had been promoted but ordinary was all I needed. This house was a souped-up version of that, up-to-date and five minutes from the woods. On the doorstep we put on our 'nothing has happened' faces and were greeted by the owners: only a little older than us but surprisingly square. She was all Crimplene and Nylon, and her awkward, blow-away hair needed a cut. He wore a beige sleeveless pullover that couldn't claim to be a tank top, and Eric Morecambe glasses. They were formal; their handshakes felt as if they belonged in an office. Clive and June Hollis, I'd remembered, knowing John would forget. Smokers – I knew that as soon as I stepped inside. This would be a quick once-over and we'd make a hasty exit.

Some of the wallpaper was bright and trendy, although I've never cared for orange. I made a few polite noises but they didn't allow for many questions or seem to have a lot of time to waste on details. I didn't mind that, or the questions they didn't ask us: *"Do you have any children?"* Some of my friends would have called the kitchen "super" and it was certainly full of gadgets, but then I didn't suppose the Soda Stream or Hostess trolley would be included in the price. In the master bedroom John seemed impressed. I wasn't sure whether that was down to the oversized Teasmade on the bedside unit or the brand new en-suite bathroom with bold geometrics on the plastic curtain. For me it was all too neat, like a display at one of those new DIY places bigger than cathedrals where people flocked on Sundays.

After a quick glance into the ultra-coordinated second bedroom, the Hollises were moving us on downstairs when John pointed out, "Isn't there a third bedroom?"

"Bomb site at the moment," said Mr Hollis. He grinned. "June's idea of decorating."

"Do you mind?" she reacted, but it all felt a bit stiff.

We headed downstairs and declined tea, only partly because they obviously hoped we would. As John reversed very carefully out of their drive I was surprised to see Mr Hollis running out in his slippers. John wound down the window.

"Maybe we could come and see your place? You haven't got a buyer yet?"

And John started with a promising, "Well …" but pretty much agreed, in principle. After suggesting that it would be so much cheaper and easier if we could come to a private arrangement, Mr Hollis scuttled back and I waited a moment before I launched my protest as John pulled onto the road.

"Who does a house swap? We didn't even go to a party and leave our keys in the ashtray! And the place stinks of fags. It's chozzy."

"Oh, I don't know …"

That was when I looked back at the house for no particular reason and saw the face at the upstairs window, small but beautiful under a big straw hat.

"Darling!" I breathed, because the girl was young and sad. "They have a child. Why did they lie?"

John pointed out that no one mentioned children, us or them, and we weren't liars. But we agreed how odd it was that they didn't even open the door of that third bedroom an inch or two. It wasn't long before a total of months in front of *The Rockford Files*, *Kojak* and *Paul Temple* started to have an effect on John's thinking.

"Have any children gone missing around here lately?" he asked. "You read the local paper."

"What? You think they're kidnappers now. A moment ago you wanted to have them round for tea."

He said he supposed she could be a niece visiting. I said in that case she would have been drawing at the dining table or watching *Tom and Jerry* on TV.

"This girl," he began, and paused. "She was … real?"

At that point I slumped and cried. Because I knew about ghosts at windows, and I would have loved to see Adam at his, to feel him when I hoovered his room and smoothed his bed.

"The girl's alive," I said, and the word sounded angry, like an accusation. I was remembering make-up now, make-up she was too young to wear.

He reached out a moment to lay his hand on mine. "Susie," he said, "I'm just trying to understand."

And over the next few hours, I realised I felt the same.

What could we do but go back again, even if we ran the risk of raising their hopes as sellers, and inviting the estate agents to pester us?

John wanted to drop by unannounced but I said we'd better obey the rules or we'd be black-listed by every estate agent in town. Part of me wished we'd never met Mr and Mrs Hollis but the girl's face stayed with me. John wanted me to put an age on it, but didn't seem to appreciate it when I said, "Adam's age?" He was intent on sleuthing; he knew some-one from Badminton Club who was an ex-copper and not very discreet after a few drinks. In the meantime we made an appointment through the estate agents to return on the Tuesday evening. Apparently the Hollises couldn't have any viewings over the weekend, which John said was suspicious in itself.

I left him to his detective work over beers and felt a bit resentful that he'd only missed one week's Badminton and one Sunday at the pub, while I'd shed everything, including weight. Telling myself we had our own ways of surviving, I gave myself up to frenzied cooking and cleaning with *The Archers* and *Desert Island Discs*, and found myself hungry for news when he came home.

When he said, "No girls have gone missing round here in the last year," I told him we must be glad about that. He fell asleep after lunch with his head tilting forward on the sofa, and I stroked the hair tapering down the back of his neck, like I used to stroke Adam's.

John missed the train home on Tuesday so we were late for our repeat viewing and rather on edge – but our scratchiness was nothing compared with Mr Hollis's unsmiling reception, glancing down at his watch.

"June is in bed now, I'm afraid. Under the weather," he said, "so shall we make it brief? I expect you want to see the third bedroom, check on progress?"

He led us upstairs without waiting for an answer or reacting to John's apology for being late. Or my expressed concern for Mrs Hollis, even though I had little patience with people's readiness to be ill. The door to the master bedroom was closed and I wondered whether I should be tiptoeing in my stockinged feet. We crept past it to the small, narrow bedroom that had been unfit to glimpse a few days earlier, and even from the landing, the smell of the magnolia emulsion through the open door was strong. There was a white built-in wardrobe that seemed to have been marked during decorating but the rest of the furniture, including a single bed, was covered with dust sheets. John commented that Mrs Hollis had "done a good job." Then looking back at the window sill, I noticed something that looked like a small green toy sitting beside a spider plant.

Ushered on, we were told, "Feel free to remind yourselves of the downstairs rooms."

We kept that cursory, probably with the same comments on the same features. John sounded quite convincing when he said we just needed to talk things through before we jumped in.

"Well don't waste time," Mr Hollis said. "We've found somewhere ourselves, offer accepted, green light. We don't want to lose it."

Back in the car, John said anyone would think he had a plane to catch. I looked back but no face at the window. The curtains in the master bedroom were drawn but they didn't block out the light that went on as we drew away.

"I don't believe she's ill," I said.

"You mean it's like a bedtime headache." He looked at me, tender and apologetic. We hadn't made love since our fervent clinging the night Adam died. "I can't imagine them ... can you?"

For a second we grinned like schoolkids over smut. When I told him about the toy I couldn't be sure whether he was sceptical or excited.

"What kind of toy?"

"I couldn't see. Something very small. Like a pencil topper."

There were toys in Adam's room, just a couple of old favourites. Could the Hollises be in mourning too? John would say that was too big a coincidence and even though I couldn't have spelled Psychology in those days I knew grief could twist everything into a new shape.

It seemed we had no explanation, and no plan either. Then early the next evening a young couple came to view our house. She was five months pregnant, and a slip of a thing with the beginnings of a bump; he was protective, in a *Starsky* cardi with curls to match. It's hard not to be delighted when nice, glowing people fall in love with your home.

"Well," John hesitated, looking at me.

"We're going to make an offer on a place we viewed a second time yesterday," I said. Because of the woods, I think. Because I couldn't face starting again, with other people and other houses, when the Hollis place was a change and that was all that mattered. And I couldn't walk away from the child, not without knowing.

"Oh," said the young woman in our hallway, "it would be so lovely if it worked out." Slipping into her shoes and steadied by his arm, she asked, "How old is your ... daughter?"

"Son," said John. "Nearly nine. A good boy."

We smiled like proud parents should, and closed the door. John expressed astonishment and I shrugged.

"Why not? There's nothing much wrong with the house, once you take its owners out of the equation." We debated whether the adjective should be Hitchcockian or Hitchcockesque. And I imagine Nilsson wailed as loudly in John's head as mine.

In an unconscious way I liked both ideas: our dead house resurrected and smelling of Baby Powder again, and the Hollis place with its double-glazed windows wide open to get rid of something more than smoke. In bed we talked about what would fit where, and buying some garden furniture to sit near the roses in summer. There might be room for the pond that hadn't seemed safe when Adam was small. We were both fond of frogs, still are.

Things moved faster after that than we could have foreseen. Both offers were accepted, and our chain looked as if it might hold. We still speculated or joked about the dark secret we might soon uncover but also about our own imaginations. Although I didn't mention it to John, I began to think about trying again, before too long, for a baby. Somehow there had to be a future. It was what Adam had told me, after the third miscarriage, when he was only six and I was crying: "There's always hope, Mummy."

In between sorting out a few cupboards, I even looked for jobs within a bus ride from the Hollis house, circling a few in the local paper and telling myself to make some calls. But as school run time drew closer that afternoon, I acted on a mad impulse. I ordered a taxi and asked the driver to drop me a few hundred yards away. I didn't wear dark glasses or pull up the collar of my mac, just strolled towards the house, half-expecting to see a girl ride her bike back from school – until I remembered that we'd seen no bike, no child's coat on a hook, no small shoes in the hall.

The house seemed quiet. No Morris Marina in the drive. I almost hurried back home, questioning my own sanity. Instead I walked up to the yellow front door and rang the bell, thinking not very productively about what to say if June opened the door with a suspicious squint.

She didn't. Someone else did.

The face was round and pretty but the hair was badly cut into a short back and sides. The lips were smeared as if to clear the shiny red away. The dress that hung down to the child's ankles was too loose and too adult. The bare feet were decorated with pearly pink nail varnish – I'd seen it on June's well-manicured fingernails. The brown eyes were wide and thickly lashed.

"Please, can I stay here with you? They don't want me. They call me Keith."

Over the next five minutes of restlessly watching the drive and the clock – both of us – I learned more than I'd ever imagined about how a child could feel about being in the wrong body. And how ashamed, cruel and cunning parents could be. She told me she was home-schooled and never saw other children unless her cousins came, when they went to the Beeches and she had to pretend to be a real boy. She didn't go out much; her parents didn't want people to see her as a girl and she didn't want to be seen any other way. So they only allowed her to play in the back garden when the neighbours were away. And sometimes, when they couldn't trust her, they locked her in her room.

"I'm not a bad child."

I put my hand on her shoulder and she cried, just a tear or two down her cheek disturbing the powder. "You're not. You're yourself, that's all."

She told me she didn't want to move because of the woods – and showed me how you could just see the tops of the trees from the window. And because of the friends who lived in her room. She showed me the smallest, the toy from the window sill: a tiny rubbery mermaid with a bendy tail called Millie.

"Where is your mother now?"

"She's at the hairdressers. She won't let me grow mine."

"Will she be long?"

"Ten minutes maybe."

"Where's the phone?" I asked. "I need to call my husband."

She made me tea, and wanted me to have a biscuit, her "favourite" Jammie Dodger, and I told her they were my son's too. She was so sad to hear we'd lost him that I hugged her.

"What shall I call you?" I asked her.

"Steph," she said.

That's the part I remember most clearly. How I held her hand a moment as her mother came through the door. How brave she was, and clear, as if somehow she knew we'd love her. The rest of it is a blur: the ratio of diplomacy, on our part, to accusations and threats; how long before John arrived; how we drove through it all as if we didn't care about rules or red tape. Just Steph: the only detail they didn't care about at all. They'd tried to "help him", they insisted. "He" was "unnatural" and "out of control". And all the while she played with the mermaid, quietly narrating her adventures, making her swim. We managed some bluster about Social Services with rather loose use of the word "adoption" and all defences were dropped. It was as if we'd come to tell them they'd won on the Pools. But at the same time I could tell they despised us: no morals, no shame.

"We didn't have you down for perverts," her father said.

For a couple of months I called each day and put those carefree years at Teacher Training College to good use – taking with me some pretty notebooks so my pupil could write Stephanie Jameson on the covers. It was a different world, of course. Without the Worldwide Web, a London teenager could deliver a baby and sneak it off to Gran in Middlesborough without 'authorities' banging on any doors. Even so, I do wonder whether without the chorus in our heads, we would have dared. We weren't in our right minds.

Our Adam really did hold us together, John and me and Steph. And she loves him too. She still says she's proud of us, calls me "feisty" and a "pioneer". Now my Twitter account says LGBT but my best guess back then would have been Larry Grayson's Bad Television. So when she insists I was ahead of my time, it makes me smile because up to that point I'm not sure I'd ever been a free thinker in my life. And I wouldn't have said that buying a child represents the pinnacle of enlightenment in this murky world, but no one can tell me it was wrong all the same.

They say moving house is one of the most stressful things you ever do, and Steph and her magical friends didn't have to. It's still her home, whenever she likes. John asks each breakfast time, "Is our Steph coming today?" He's forgotten most of the newer things so he doesn't always remember she's married now and sometimes refers to Adam as her brother. Which in a way he is; she's got to know him so well.

When she arrives with her Ravi, John's so excited to see her.

"Here she is," he cries, and echoes her words from forty years ago: "Included, like the carpets."

You can find out more about the authors* who have read and reviewed a story in this collection at the end of the book.

Like all good fairy tales, The Brute and the Beast *has unexpected twists that delight the reader; it is also veined with startling imagery. A heart-warmer of a story about beauty, greed, different types of love and, ultimately, salvation.*

Nuala O'Connor, author*, Ireland

The Brute and the Beast *is beautifully written and I enjoyed the humour in how Bute got his name. The story is about finding the beauty, kindness and generosity to love – and the ending surprised me!*

Michelle Kok, Masters student, Brisbane, Australia

The Brute and the Beast *is an interesting story which can be read on many levels, a fairy tale and a parable. It tells us that people who are beautiful can be totally beastly, things don't make us happy, people don't always look beyond the obvious and Nature is a great healer. There is also a deeper, religious level to this story, about valuing the spiritual rather than earthly things.*

Jill Hipson, BSL teacher, Hertfordshire, UK

The Brute and the Beast *is a lovely story, where beauty is not everything. It is not the outer beauty that counts, but the inner beauty in your heart.*

Pauline Rowntree, student, Bedfordshire, UK

This is an exquisite retelling of a traditional tale with fresh twists to the text of Bute's life and love. Utterly absorbing and lyrically told, the story perfectly captures fairy tale narrative whilst giving it a new perspective.

Clare Anstee, teaching assistant, Herts UK

I loved the underlying story of beauty not being in the eye of the beholder. The Brute and the Beast *is wonderfully written with an abundance of fantastic details and adjectives to let the mind visualise the scenes and personalities in the book.*

Susan Barker-Mewis, HR Consultant, Saltaire, West Yorkshire, UK

The Brute and the Beast

In a dark, stone castle under an angry sky, a baby joined the world – and gave it a powerful kick. But the moment they saw him, his parents put a sudden end to the celebrations. A shocked silence fell like a shroud over everything and everywhere they owned.

Since they were a dashing Count and elegant Countess, these parents even owned the people who rented their cottages and worked their land. So this baby was born into wealth and power. A lace-trimmed crib and silver rattle awaited him. Before he gave his first orders, the villagers were ready to bow and curtsey at the sound of his name.

This infant was a healthy boy with strong lungs and even stronger limbs. But he was enormous – so huge, in fact, that his mother almost died giving birth to him. He was also enormously ugly. The matted black hair sprouting from his massive head reminded his mother of a dead crow, his nose was as wide and flat as a lamb chop and the mouth that widened in a howl was wide enough to admit the whole lamb.

His mother stared at him in horror.

"Eaagh! He's a brute!" she cried. "Take him away!"

The Count agreed that the boy wasn't handsome. But his size might have its advantages. No one would cross such a brute, cheat him or get in his way. Already his grip was crab-like.

Honoria, his mother, stayed in bed on the day of his christening, but she gave orders that Brute was his name. There was no point in calling him Tristan or Lancelot, or even James or William. Honoria believed in calling a spade a spade.

But on the birth certificate, there was no r. Maybe the Count wasn't good at spelling. So the boy's name was Bute.

By the time Bute was four he could reach up to pat his mother on the head. Or would have done, if she'd allowed him near enough. And although he grew as tough as the roots of trees, he seemed at first to be as gentle as a violet on the woodland floor. His father took him walking when the forests were quietest. Bute loved those violets that tried to hide, the primroses, bluebells and wood anemones. He watched the deer and rabbits, and gazed up awestruck at the falcons and hawks circling and swooping. Quick and determined, Bute could climb the mountains in less time than it took many children to cross a stream. And at the top, he liked to stand like a giant, beaten by air under sun as he overlooked the land that would be his.

He never mixed with other children, except his cousin Kareen, who was many years older than Bute. She read him stories and taught him to draw. Her visits every summer were the happiest times of each year. He never went into the village, to the market, to the fair, to church or to school. His mother hid him away from eyes that would look on him with disgust, or fear.

"No one will marry him," she told the Count. "And when we're gone, what will happen to our fortune?"

Bute's father Tiron did not want to think. He enjoyed his son's company, but he knew the world would not.

Meanwhile Bute kept on growing. He learned from a tutor in the castle, and made friends with the servants (who were paid not to grimace or scream). By the time he was ten, he had started to press hard against the bars of his invisible cage.

Kareen would soon be married and no longer visited. Bute wanted friends to play with. There were children in the village. He saw them from the castle windows, swimming in the lake, kicking a ball, running and chasing, climbing trees.

One day he waved, and shouted so loudly that the boys below looked up, and saw him. One ran, as if a pack of wolves rushed growling after him. The rest stared. They pulled faces that were almost as ugly as his.

"You can't catch us, Beast!" shouted one, and threw a stone that fell short.

Bute didn't understand, but he felt a fist harden and shook it at them. A growling noise throbbed in his throat and the boys screamed and fled. But others came, on other days, dared by their friends to catch a glimpse of him, and every time they pulled their faces and jeered at him, his anger grew.

Until one day he burst into his mother's bedroom and seized her mirror by its golden handle.

What he felt, at the sight of his face, was rage. He slammed the mirror down on Honoria's dressing table. She shrieked as dagger blades of glass fell jagged on the floor.

The next morning, he woke to find his mother had gone. Taking her finest dresses, bonnets and jewels, she had gone to live with her sister in a castle over the mountains. Full of grief, the Count blamed Bute.

He no longer felt the smallest pride in his colossal son. His muscles and his vigour meant nothing now. He was monstrous, and he was dangerous too. For father and son, there were no more walks in the dawn or the twilight. Only when Bute played the viol or the flute, and the Count closed his eyes, did they both forget for a moment the ugliness and the shame.

As for Bute's anger, it was buried deep inside. Like the shards of glass it pressed its tip on his heart. Only when he wandered alone with flowers and animals did the pricking stop. He looked in no more mirrors. He learned to use a sword and a bow, and to ride the most powerful stallion in the land. With a deafening cry that sent children running for their cottages, he built his strength by hurling logs. Grunting and groaning, he found he could push his father's carriage down the hill – so fast that he must throw himself down after it and block it like a wall.

So when his father died one night, because his carriage plunged off the rocky path into the lake, Bute felt angry – with himself, with the horses, with the path and the water. His mother came to the funeral, but then she rode away again, to marry a duke.

Bute was only twenty, but he was Count Bute now.

It was days after his father died that Bute first glimpsed Trusanne. What he saw, early one morning in the forest, was something more beautiful, more graceful and delicate than any deer. A young girl was picking flowers, and placing them carefully in hair that seemed to gleam like a summer cloud full of sunlight.

As she lifted her face at the sound of his heavy tread on branches, he saw her beauty. She was so lovely that Bute was sure the lakes that presented her reflection must ripple with delight. The breeze must breathe a sigh of pleasure every time it brushed her cheeks.

He did not dare let her see him, in case she screamed and ran. From behind a huge tree he watched her, and smiled at the lightness of her feet and the softness of her skin. Returning to the castle, he felt her brightness in each dark corner. When he closed his eyes that night, he smelt the flowers she carried.

But how could he speak to her? How could he take one step towards her without frightening her away? Bute told himself she was lost to him forever, like a rare bird glimpsed before it flew. For the first time for many years, he looked once more at his face, distorted in the silver lid of a box on his shelf. Grabbing the box, he threw it out of his open window, and heard it land in the lake. There it would sink into mud. Bute gripped his heavy neck as if to squeeze out his own breath. But he knew that he could never separate himself from the face he showed the world. He could not bury or drown it. Yet it was not him.

And whoever the girl might be, she could never be his.

As Trusanne returned to the bare, damp cottage with an armful of flowers, her father had only one question.

"Did he see you?"

Trusanne gave him a small, satisfied smile.

"He did."

Her father, who lay ill and weak on a mattress on the earth floor, lifted both fists and shook them in a gesture of triumph.

"Then the trap is laid!" he cried, and wheezed. "Water, girl!"

She brought him a chipped cup and he drank desperately. She wondered how much longer he could live. Her rescue could not come soon enough.

"He is grotesque," she said, for out of the corner of her eye she had seen enough, "a monster."

"A monster with a fortune that's bigger than he is!"

Trusanne could see no other way. There were plenty of young men in the village who were handsome or charming, or made her laugh. She was sure that every one of them would be glad to make her their wife, but none of them could give her pearls and rubies, velvet, silk and lace.

Even before Bute saw Trusanne a second time, he loved her. For weeks he glimpsed her from a distance, sometimes following her with a cloak around his head, or watching from behind a wall when she bought bread at the market.

Trusanne did not have the patience to wait for him to speak. Her father was too ill now to work at all. Spitting and coughing, weak and sharp, he was counting on her. The next time she walked in the dew by the lake, she heard Bute taking shelter in the bushes around the shore, and turned.

"Don't hide, sir," she said, though the sight of him was like a bad taste, or a worse smell. She curtseyed, and lowered her eyes as if she were innocent, or shy.

Bute bowed. It was hard to find words, but he told her who he was and where he lived. She seemed surprised.

When she told him her father was ill, he said he would send his doctor.

"I can buy medicine, sir, if only you would lend me ..."

He pressed gold coins into her hand. Overjoyed, she thanked him and hurried away.

Trusanne bought a handful of herbs at the market to mash to a paste for her father, and ordered from the seamstress a black satin dress edged with silver thread, and a light gauze veil that barely hid her face. She would be the most beautiful daughter in mourning the village had ever seen, and leave the foolish Count quite breathless – and helpless too.

Indeed, the herbs were too little too late. When word reached Bute that her father had died, he could not bear to think of Trusanne living alone in the moss-walled cottage with its tin roof that flapped in the wind. There he visited her, bowing his head and bending his chest to enter.

When she lifted her veil, her beauty was astonishing. As she looked at him with pity for herself, he thought her tender. He longed to make her happy.

"Will you marry me?" he asked. "Everything I own, every mountain, forest, river and seashore, will be yours. And you will wear a dress edged with gold."

Trusanne opened her mouth, but now that their plan had succeeded so easily, it was harder to answer. She had no wish to stay in the cottage and break her nails digging up carrots. But even the bumpiest, muddiest potatoes were prettier than Bute.

Trusanne had a better idea. "I thank you, sir," she said, "but I am just sixteen, and deeply shocked. I fear I cannot think clearly."

"I understand," said Bute. "But while you consider, let me look after you. Let me see you at my breakfast table. I have many spare rooms in my castle. Choose one, and I shall fill it with flowers."

So Trusanne chose three: one for sleeping, one for her reading and sewing, and one for all the dresses Bute gave her. She came to live at the castle, but she kept her eyes on the mirrors and the tapestries, the fireplace and the china. Those eyes did not meet his. Bute thought what she felt was grief, and modesty. But it was disgust.

For now that he was fully grown, Bute was a great, bumpy hill of a man. He was knotty to the touch, his skin thick and woody. His eyebrows were tangled as nests. Matted hair fell dull and heavy to his shoulders and bristled out of his jutting chin like thorns. He always looked as if he had been in a fight, but of course, he never had. No one would dare fight Bute. And Bute's heart was much too forgiving to hold a grudge against anyone – except himself.

As Trusanne slept that first night, Bute sat below in the great hall and hoped he could take care of Trusanne forever. The fires were stoked to keep her warm. He'd hung the richest velvet curtains and picked enough roses, white, cream, pink and red, to decorate every windowsill. Her wardrobe was full of the finest gowns, and he'd left a jewelled box of ribbons and combs, rings and bracelets, beside her bed.

In the morning, Bute woke before her and carried her breakfast on a silver tray. He stirred the porridge himself until it was creamy smooth. He baked the bread, kneading the dough with his own (clean) hands.

"Ew! Too sweet!" she said, and spat out the porridge.

She began to shiver.

"It's cold," she said.

Nothing was right for Trusanne. The rugs, the shawls, the couch and the bedspread were the wrong size, shape or colour. Her shoes were too tight or too loose, too slippery or too stiff. Her rooms were too dark by day and too bright by night.

He gave her a silver bucket to take to the well. She said it was too heavy. Furious with his own stupidity, he hurled it onto the fire.

She complained that the jewelled ribbons he threaded through her hair made her head ache.

"Forgive me, sweetest," Bute begged her. "I'll get it right next time."

Bute understood. She was delicate. She had taste, where he had none. He changed everything she did not like, again and again, and told her how sorry he was that he had made a mistake.

When she said she was going out, to a ball or a party, he waved her off in the polished carriage. He watched the white horses canter away into the night, scarlet ribbons plaited into their tails. Of course, thought Bute, she liked to dance, and it wouldn't be fair to spoil her fun with his great, clumsy feet that never knew where to tread. But sometimes, when she'd gone, he growled at himself, and bit his teeth into his thick, puffy lips until they were thicker and puffier.

"Forgive me," he told his servants. "I didn't mean to frighten you."

But they were not frightened of Bute. They only hoped he would never know how his bride-to-be spoke of him when he was not there. And they argued over what he would do if he ever overheard her call him a brute and a beast, a fool and an embarrassment. For his rage would be wilder than a storm on the mountains.

While she was out walking in sunshine, Bute carved wooden birds for her to find. They were so light they looked ready to fly, and so real the breeze tried to lift their feathers. Trusanne never spoke of them. Sometimes he wondered where she kept them all.

Trusanne was always too tired to talk when she came home late from a party. But Bute waited up for her, so that he could play her a lullaby on the flute or viol. Although he watched her by candlelight till she fell asleep, he dared not kiss her goodnight. He would hate to scratch her with his bark-like lips. And he dared not stroke her hair, for fear of catching it in his thick, rough fingers and tugging it.

Bute was sad to see Trusanne frown. He blamed himself and would do anything to smooth the snag in her beauty.

"Can we have a ball here, dear Bute?" she asked him, sweetly.

"Of course!" he cried, delighted, and hired the finest musicians.

A few nights later the castle was full of guests. Trusanne had sent the invitations, but Bute was surprised to find no girls she had known at school, and none of her cousins or old neighbours from the village. She had even forgotten his own cousin, Kareen, even though he had reminded her how kind she had been when he was a boy. Instead she had asked the richest lords and ladies in the land – along with a few young men who danced well enough to partner her.

Bute sat in the minstrels' gallery and looked down, clapping and tapping his feet. He watched Trusanne dance most of all with Harin, the baker, who made her laugh and smile, and never once trod on her toes.

After the ball was over, Trusanne shed tears.

"My feet are sore!" she complained, so Bute fetched a bowl of warm water scented with lavender.

He smiled down on her. "Soon, perhaps, there will be another party in the castle – to celebrate our wedding."

Trusanne sighed. He could see she was too weary to think of anything but sleep.

"Rest, dear," he told her, and left her in peace.

The next day, Trusanne called at the baker's.

"Marry me," whispered Harin, as he sold her a warm bread roll, but Trusanne only laughed. He had no castle. All he could offer was a hot oven stacked with bread and cakes.

Bute's cousin Kareen and her husband, Yarl, came to visit, but Trusanne did not seem pleased to see them. Yarl was overweight and had a beard she thought nasty. Kareen was old enough to be her mother and Trusanne told her maids she had no grace or style. She yawned at the dinner table as if she had never been so bored.

"She is shallow," Kareen told him afterwards, when Trusanne was in bed, "and cares for no one but herself."

Bute would not hear a word against her. He made excuses for her rudeness.

"She's just a girl," he said, "and was not brought up to be gracious."

"Did she remember your birthday?" asked Kareen, and Bute hung his head. "I thought not!"

Waking the next day to find their guests still there, Trusanne pulled faces behind her back.

"Will the hag stay forever?" she asked.

Bute was shocked. His fingers tightened into his palms. But he told himself it was playfulness. She was still so young.

At the end of the visit, Kareen thanked Bute for his kindness. In the castle doorway she took his hands. While Trusanne turned away, horrified at the idea of a goodbye kiss, Kareen whispered, "She will break your heart."

But Bute only hoped he would not break hers, for nothing he did could bring to her face the light he had seen in it when she danced with Harin the baker.

He did not know that she had broken Harin's heart already. Then one evening when she rode back from town, she ran up to her rooms and flung herself on her four poster bed. He heard her crying and it stirred him to wildness inside.

Bute knocked on her door but she told him to go away.

"Are you sick, dearest?"

"Leave me alone!"

Bute kicked the wall outside her door. Then he breathed deeply all the way down to the kitchens, where he asked the servants to take her fresh buttered bread and a slice of black cherry cake.

"The baker's is empty, sir," said the cook.

"So's the baker," said the groom.

"Harin's gone, sir," said the maid, "for good."

Bute was sorry to hear the news, but not just because he liked Harin's pastries. He knew how much Trusanne liked to dance with the light-footed baker whose smile was so boyish and whose hair was so glossy when he bowed his head.

He asked the maid to open the windows in Trusanne's bedroom so that she could see the sunshine and hear the birdsong over the mountains. But the girl returned with a bruise on her scalp. Trusanne had thrown a golden hairbrush at her head.

The days went by but Trusanne stayed in her rooms. She ate the cherries Bute picked for her but sent no thanks. She wore the dress with diamonds at its cuffs and hems but Bute was not permitted to see for himself how it fitted. Only the servants knew what made her sick at heart.

The grooms and gardeners agreed that in Harin's place, they too would have run as far as they could.

"The poor Count can't see what's staring him in the face," said one of Trusanne's maids. "She should be ashamed of herself."

But only one person in the castle was ashamed. Ashamed that he could not dance well enough to partner her. Ashamed that his manners were so oafish and his looks so grim. Ashamed that he could not please her no matter how hard he tried.

Through the door he called, asking what she needed. "Let's be married, dearest," he said. "You know how you love a party. You can plan it all, every beautiful detail."

"Leave me alone!" she cried, and he heard something – perhaps one of her delicate shoes – thud against the door.

When she emerged at last, it was only to pout and sulk. She seemed tired of everything. Anxiously, he followed her up the steps to her rooms.

"What can I do," asked Bute, "to make you happy?"

"Nothing," she muttered, sitting down at her dressing table to look in the mirror rimmed with pearls.

"What can I do differently?" he persisted. "I can learn to dance. I can cut my hair. I can improve my manners. I'll change ..."

"You can't," she told him, brushing her hair in the mirror. She looked up at his image towering behind her, thick and ugly as a chimney. "You can't change *that.*"

Now at last Bute understood. How stupid he had been! How foolish to imagine, how deluded! She could not bear the sight of him. He told her he could not be the husband she wanted, and would not keep her there in the castle against her will.

"Go where you must," he said, "and find happiness. Take whatever you need. I will make sure you never go without anything. And I will be here, if ever you wish to return."

Her beautiful smile returned. There were many things she needed; he promised she should have them all. Her gladness was good to see. Bute felt a guilty sorrow that he had trapped her there where she could not be happy.

The next day, Bute pressed into her hands a velvet purse heavy with gold coins. Then she rode away on his best white horse, laden with goblets and vases, gowns and jewels, ornaments and mirrors.

"Goodbye," she said, but she did not look back.

In the castle doorway, Bute felt a surge inside him like a wave that would drown everything in its path. His mouth broke open in a groan that was also a roar. He charged like a bull at the nearest tree, and pushed his head against its trunk. His feet kicked its base and roots. Like branches in a hurricane, his arms flailed and beat the flies in the air, the bark, his chest and head.

Running back into the castle, he burst into the room where Trusanne used to sleep, and looking at the figure in the long glass, splintered it with his fist. Bute licked the blood from his knuckles. She hated him, almost as much as he hated himself.

But every morning Bute crept into her bedroom hoping to find her asleep. Every night before he drew the curtains he gazed out over the mountains, hoping to glimpse her in the distance, riding back to him. Under her bed, he found a tumbling pile of all the wooden birds he'd carved for her. Bute cried silently as his big, thick fingers stroked away the dust that skimmed their wings.

The castle felt too big and too silent without dancing feet. He made himself a home in a cave nearby: a safe, dark place where he could not frighten children. He foraged for berries and nuts, fruit and leaves, and smiled his thanks when a villager brought him something baked and sweet, or warming and spicy.

To his servants who came to visit he said, "You're welcome. Please sit. But bring me nothing. There is nothing I need."

For weeks he spent his days under a rocky roof, thinking, remembering and wishing, playing tunes to soothe his own rage. Then one morning he told himself he was the Count, washed in the stream, removed the twigs from his hair and returned to his castle.

Suddenly feeling hungry, he slipped into the kitchens to surprise the servants. But what he overheard put an end to his appetite.

"Madam is to marry her baker, then."

"In a village just over the lake."

"May they be happy! A fine pair they'll make!"

"Let's hope the Count doesn't hear of it, bless him!"

"He'd shower them with wedding gifts, poor fool!"

They turned at the sound of heavy steps. Bute was running, knocking obstacles from his path. Down the hill he sped, leaping rocks and winding through trees until he reached the lake. In he dived, and swam faster than he had ever needed to swim. Exhausted, he dragged himself up on the other side, clutching reeds and gasping. His body felt heavier than ever, his clothes sodden and starting to steam in the sun. Squinting, he gazed towards the village and a church spire rising beyond the brightness into cloud. He forced himself on.

At the sound of bells rippling, he covered his ears, holding his head tight between his hands. Was she married already, and not to him? He did not know why he had come. Why must he put his hand in the fire? The servants were right: he was a fool.

From the bushes at the edge of the churchyard he watched, well hidden, as Trusanne stepped outside. Bute saw the beauty of the bride, wearing a dress fit for a duchess. He smelt the flowers she carried: enough lilies, irises for a royal grave. Bute had paid for her to marry another man.

Stooping in case she glimpsed his head rising above a gorse bush, he heard laughter – the bride's the clearest and highest of all. Then the wedding party crossed the churchyard towards a house, grander than its neighbours, its door marked by a wreath of flowers. It was the home he had paid for, where she would live with Harin the baker, and gaze lovingly at his handsome face.

The villagers filed inside and following at a distance, Bute heard gasps of astonishment and admiration.

"Stained glass," Trusanne told them as she welcomed them all in. "And the floor is marble. Please remove your shoes."

Bute was not invited. Tired now, Bute sat under a tree overlooking the baker's house. Guests moved outside into the garden with its paths and borders, statues and arches, and a lily pond with a cherub on its fountain. No village wife had ever had such elegance and style, and as he watched he saw envy in the whispers behind hands.

Bute's clothes were stiff on his aching body. He could not have felt wearier or emptier if he had been beaten at the whipping post. The last traces of his hope had been stolen and without it he did not know who he was or why. He turned away and began to stumble home.

But before he reached the lake he heard a laughter that jeered. Bute stopped. Were they mocking her? Were they spoiling her day and poisoning her triumph? He took a few paces back towards the party, close enough to see a ring of guests gathered around something thick as a tree trunk and taller than a man, yet not human. But what was it, this thing they clapped as they danced, bowing and curtseying before it? Not a scarecrow either, though branches angled up and out of its bulk and a hat sat on its head. Stepping to one side Bute glimpsed through the circle as a man bent to pick up a chicken bone to hurl. Harin, laughing, drunk already. His target was a giant of sacking and wood.

"Count," mocked Harin, doffing his hat to the giant. "You get more handsome every day."

The laughter roared like fire.

"Come, wife!" called Harin. "Come and curtsey to the dashing Count! He wants to dance with you!"

"Mind your toes, Trusanne!" yelled someone as she made her way through the circle. She stared at the figure, and put her hands on her waist.

"I'll never curtsey to *that* again!"

Whether she spat, or hurled a shoe at the lumpy head, Bute would never know. With his heart squeezed like a lemon, and laughter chasing him on the wind, he ran until he could no longer hear his name. Up the mountain he charged, towards the castle, and as he reached its walls he bellowed a wordless cry.

It was a warning. The servants did not wait to ask what they could bring their master, but fled to the village.

Alone in the great hall, Bute kicked aside benches as if they were pebbles under his feet. He hurled his own chair into the fire and watched as the flames melted velvet and turned gold to syrup.

Wrenching a sword from the wall where it hung, he sliced the head from a statue. The head of a goddess, whose pose Trusanne had liked to copy, thudded down in one piece. It rolled to a stop, upright on the floor as if the rest of it had been buried up to the neck in stone.

With the tip of the sword he speared a tapestry she had never liked, and bundled it into the fire. Bute looked at the sword in his hand and bent it over his thigh like a twig.

He took an axe to a chest he'd carved for her and sliced it like ham.

He pulled the silver hands from the clock above the chimney and knuckled a fist through its face.

Seizing a precious vase, he threw it at the stone floor where it cracked apart like an egg with a ferocious chick. Down beside it he dragged the polished shield that bore his coat of arms, rattling like a pan.

Then he charged the high table where his parents used to feast with their important guests. Chest barrelled, he knocked it over onto its side. One by one he wrenched off its legs as if they were no thicker than the bones of a roasted chicken. Left with the table top, thick and wide and long as a cottage garden, he pushed it to the wall where it beat ornaments thudding and tinkling from shelves.

Bute was breathless now, but still stone pillars supported the roof. He wrapped his arms around one and leaned back, tugging, until his face was scarlet. It would take an army to pull down the walls. He was spent, his chest sinking. The cage was still a cage and the prisoner was not free.

Bute fell to his knees, his arms across his chest and his head down.

"Sir?"

He did not turn at first, imagining the voice to be in his head. Not Trusanne. Not his mother. In the surface of the shield settled now on the floor he saw his own face, mouth gaping, eyes raw. More mis-shapen than ever.

But behind it was another face, curved on the copper, small and unreal. A woman brought him water. She moved slowly. Her eyes did not look away.

"Who are you?" he asked.

"My name is Dia."

As Bute drank, he saw the blood run from his torn hand down the stem of the goblet. It dripped on the floor.

He realised she did not see it. But as he watched her face he saw her smell it. She took a handkerchief from her pocket and, finding his hand, wrapped it around it.

"You are blind," he said.

"My world is blackness," she said, "with stabs of light."

Like mine, thought Bute. Then he felt ashamed. This woman was plainly dressed. She had no castle, no mansion, no servants, no silver or gold. And she could not see the hawks soar or the anemones open to the morning.

"You cannot see me?"

"I see your height and your strength," she said. "I see your hurt."

"Forgive me," said Bute, looking around him at everything he had smashed, twisted, snapped, torn, burned or crushed.

Through the open door a child ran to her mother, and pressed her face into her stomach.

"I frightened you," Bute told the back of her head, "Please forgive me."

"This is Asha," her mother told him. She took the girl's hand. "She is my eyes. Asha, curtsey to the Count."

The child lifted her head to look Bute in the face.

"No ..." began Bute, an arm across, fingers stretched to hide his ugliness.

Asha did not scream or grimace, or bury her head away. She studied him. Bute waited fearfully for the words that would describe his patchy, swollen skin and the nose spreading across his face like a bridge that had collapsed.

"His eyes are shiny," she reported to her mother.

Then she lifted both arms, tipping up on her toes. Bute hesitated, unable to believe what the gesture meant.

"Up?" she asked, and he scooped her high till she laughed.

Bute slept. When he woke the servants were there, as if nothing had happened and the day was like any other, but with a little more mending to do.

"Where are they?" he asked his maid. "Where are the blind woman and the girl?"

But she did not know who he meant. Bute felt panic wrap him round inside. Was he sick? Had he dreamed them? Was she a spirit come to save him from death?

But the next day, when he looked out on the hillside, he saw them, picking flowers. Suddenly Bute felt well and strong. He towered at the window, and as he smiled, she turned as if she guessed, or expected, or hoped he was there. Asha pointed and waved.

"Wait!" he yelled, his voice rolling down like a boulder. Then he followed it, almost as fast, to join them.

The afternoon was warm by the lake. Dia could smell the sun on the water. Bute picked daisies to crown Asha's head, and named the butterflies. He took them to the forest, where she heard the deer clustered behind trees before he had glimpsed them at all.

Back at the castle, Asha showed him the wooden birds he had carved for Trusanne. She sat them one by one in her mother's hands, so she could feel their beaks and feathers.

"Where do you live?" he asked her. "Do you have a husband?"

She took a long breath.

"I left him. He ..."

Seeing the light drift from her eyes, Bute frowned. "He hurt you?"

She nodded. "But ..."

Bute's chest lifted and swelled. He felt his own eyes burn. "Tell me where he is!" he cried. "I have never let my anger loose on anyone, but if ..."

She shook her head. "I am a widow," she said, "and like my husband I am at peace now."

"Peace now," echoed Asha, and took a wooden bird flying towards Bute.

He gazed around him at the empty brackets and shelves, the dents and cracks and tears that betrayed his madness.

"Peace is what I wish for you, Count."

"One, two, three!" cried Asha, tapping birds on the head, and when her mother laughed she squealed and rocked with laughter of her own.

Bute let loose his own laugh, hesitant at first, as if he lacked the practice, but surging as his shoulders rose and fell. When the laughter ebbed away at last, Asha looked from Bute to Dia as if one of them might explain what was funny.

Bute saw that Dia smelt the aroma of supper rising up from the kitchens, and invited her to stay and eat. She thanked him, and at the damaged table with its rough new legs he heard how she had journeyed south in the hope of finding work.

"I sing," she said. "It's all I can do."

"I need a singer," Bute told her, and hoped she believed him although he had not yet found a reason.

"For your peace," said Asha.

"Exactly," Bute told her, and clapped his large, thick hands. "And," he said, offering one to Asha, "I need a clown so I never forget how to laugh."

So it was that the Count took on two new members of his household.

The other servants whispered that these new duties were the hardest of all and they'd rather polish silver or carry firewood up eight flights of steps.

But the singer and the clown did not remain servants for long.

Bute decided that the castle was too big for one Count to own. Weeks later he helped a team of workmen to knock it to the ground, while at its feet they built cottages, with gardens.

"One for each of you," he told the maids who had no home without the castle.

"And one for you," he told Dia and Asha. "I too shall have a cottage, and I can't live in it without peace and laughter. So you must visit me every day."

But to his astonishment Dia shook her head. "No, Bute."

"You will not visit me?"

She reached for his hand.

"I will live with you, as your wife." She smiled, and he took her other hand, while Asha wrapped her arms around one enormous leg. "Will you marry me?"

Bute stared. She did not mock him. But then, she did not see him. She could have no idea …

"You think I do not know your face," she said. "My hands will learn it …"

"No!"

He shook his head wildly. He could not lose her too. She pressed her mouth to one hand and kissed it.

"I know all I need to know."

Bute knelt.

Asha clapped, and climbed his chest to his shoulders. "I know he's very big!" she cried, and Bute swung her up, legs dangling around his neck.

A few days before the wedding, the three of them rode to visit Kareen and Yarl, and Bute could tell by supper time that the women were friends. So when the next morning Yarl told him they had gone out in the carriage, he was glad to think of them together, whether it was dresses they were enjoying, or wildflowers. And when he was told nothing about their day, he left them to their secrets and supposed the wedding would bring a small surprise. Would his bride hold lilies of the valley, or wear a crown of ox-eye daisies?

So he was not prepared, as he waited outside the church, for the sound of horses and carriage wheels. The carriage that stopped outside the gate was elaborately painted, its wheels polished to a gleam. The finely groomed horses were so still they might have been sculpted. Bute watched as a groom in a top hat held out a gloved hand to a grand duchess who stepped out in silk. And looked straight into his eyes.

She had aged a little, but the face she wore was not so much older as new, for on it was a smile he had never seen before. She glided so hurriedly along the path that under her full gown she might have had her own wheels.

"My son!" breathed Honoria.

"Mother," said Bute, bending low to take her hand, but it was his cheek she reached to kiss – for the first time.

"How fine you look," she told him, "and with such a bride how happy you will be."

Bute stared, unable at first to understand. His mother had met Dia?

"She made me see," Honoria said, "who you are."

Bute remembered. A visit in a carriage! The wedding surprise, greater than he could have imagined! Dia's doing. Her goodness.

The Duke was behind his mother now, and gave Bute a quick bow and a gloved hand. But though he bowed politely, the bridegroom could think only of his bride. So he did not notice a slight figure watching under a tree, her fair hair hidden under a hood. He did not hear the slammed door and drunken laughter that lingered in Trusanne's head, or see the emptiness of her purse. So he could not guess at the thoughts that brought her there, or the feelings her beauty concealed.

Bute felt only his own wonder, his joy and thanks, and when Dia appeared, he knew from her smile that she saw it all.

Acknowledgements

Thank you above all to my dear editor and husband, Leslie Tate, who always sees exactly how I can improve any piece of writing – because he's a fine novelist and poet himself. These stories are stronger for his suggestions. And I love him.

I'm very grateful to new but dear friends Mark and Sheelagh for this collection's wonderful cover. Sheelagh Frew Crane captured the best of me for her portrait and Mark Crane drew on its detail for the perfectly RAVELLED cover design.

I'm thankful too to Anne at TSL for her efficiency, good humour and support with a project that means a great deal to me but is considered a risk in the world of publishing.

Finally, thanks to every reviewer for taking the time to read a story and make the comments included in this book. There are writers, librarians, teachers and booksellers among them but what they have in common is a reader's appetite, open mind and belief in stories. Almost all of them said by email that they "loved" the story they chose to read, which means just as much as the more analytical 'lit crit' in their reviews. I hope each one feels the same about the collection as a whole.

About the Author

Sue Hampton, happy these days to be known as the Bald Green Author, was born in Essex and now lives in Herts with her husband, Leslie Tate. Inspired by her father Paul and his poetry, she wrote as a curly-haired child and never stopped, even through 19 years of teaching. She also owes her lifelong love of great writing to her own English teacher Mr Smith, in the same way – although the title story in this collection is adapted from life – that Marilyn owes Mr Jones. After earning a B.Ed (hons, First Class) with English as her main, she became a primary teacher in Newham and then Herts, taking a break for her son Philip and daughter Sarah.

Her first book for children, the historical adventure *Spirit and Fire*, was published in 2007 and described by Michael Morpurgo as "enthralling … powerfully written". It was the first of many across genres and audiences. Most titles are for children or teens, but Sue also has three novels for adults: *Flashback and Purple, Aria* (e-book and audiobook) and *The Biggest Splash*, downloadable from her website. Sue is in demand as a visiting author in schools and an Ambassador for Alopecia UK. You may have seen her lead a team of bareheaded ladies to a £29,000 victory for the charity on BBC Eggheads!

Sue writes because she's fascinated by people, and by characters and relationships in fiction, and hopes to make an emotional connection as a reader and an author. She also talks about being the living proof of the power of stories, because exploring her alopecia in writing changed her life after she wrote *The Waterhouse Girl* and Michael Morpurgo described it as "beautifully written". It's a book that makes a difference. In her blogs she explores reasons to write, along with bigger ideas about diversity and individuality, activism and, of course, love.

Sue has shared her love of words with Leslie – recently on the #Purple-Tour – addressing reading and writers' groups around the country and talking in libraries and at other events. She's appeared at literary festivals like Flamstead, Alton and Lyme Regis, in the Lincoln Book Fair and

Banbury Literary Live, and helps Leslie to run a Poetry Reading Group
and mixed arts shows called Berkhamsted Live.

About the Authors who have reviewed stories in this collection

Andy Frankham-Allen is the range editor of the Lethbridge-Stewart series for Candy Jar Books and author of many things, including *Seeker*, *Beast of Fang Rock* and *Conspiracy of Silence*.

Bea Davenport is the author of two crime novels for adults, *In Too Deep* and *This Little Piggy*, and two children's novels, *The Serpent House* and *My Cousin Faustina*. She is programme leader for creative writing with the Open College of the Arts.

Billy Bob Buttons is the author of *I think I murdered Miss*, winner of the People's Book Prize 2014.

Brian Bold is the author of *Road Works*.

Dawn Finch is President of CILIP (Chartered Institute of Library and Information Professionals), a children's writer and librarian, and author of *Brotherhood of Shades* and *Skara Brae*.

Deeann Callis Graham is the author of *Head On: stories of alopecia*.

Dorothy Schwarz is the author of *Behind a Glass Wall – anatomy of a suicide*, an avian journalist, short story writer and Trustee of the Zoe Education Trust, founded in memory of her daughter.

Izzy Robertson is the author of *Dreaming the Moon*, *When Joe Met Alice* and *Catching Up With The Past*.

Karen Maitland is an author of medieval thrillers including *Company of Liars*, *The Vanishing Witch*, *The Raven's Head*, *Liars and Thieves*, *Falcons of Fire and Ice*, *The Gallows Curse* and the *Owl Killers*.

Matt Carmichael is co-author of *Spiritual Activism* with Alastair McIntosh.

Miriam Calleja is the author of *Pomegranate Heart*, a book of poetry in Maltese and English.

Nuala O'Connor is the author of *Miss Emily* (a novel about Emily Dickinson).

Robin Gregory is the author of the award-winning novel, *The Improbable Wonders of Moojie Littleman.*